Between the Flags

Between the Flags

Uncollected Stories,
1948-1990
by B.H. Friedman

Fiction Collective Two
Boulder • Normal
Brooklyn

Published by Fiction Collective Two with assistance from the New York State Council on the Arts. Additional support given by Illinois State University, the Publications Center of the University of Colorado at Boulder, Brooklyn College, and Teachers & Writers Collaborative.

Address all inquiries to: Fiction Collective Two, c/o English Department, Illinois State University, Normal Illinois 61761

The author wishes to thank the editors of publications where, sometimes in somewhat different form, the following stories appeared: "As I am You Will Be" and "Candide's Garden" *Epoch*, Summer 1948 and Fall 1980; "Whisper" *the noble savage* 4, 1961; "Did you Know Gorky? Pollock? Kline?" *Evergreen Review*, June 1967; "P__: A Case History" *Statements* 2, 1977; "Duplex" and "Mickey" *Chicago*, October 1983 and August 1985; "Eskimos" *Fiction International* 15:2, 1984; "A Dead Cousin" *Bluefish*, Spring/Summer 1987; "Search" *Manuscript*, Spring 1987; "The Couch" *Confrontation*, Spring/ Summer 1990; and "Between the Flags" *Witness*, Summer/Fall 1989. All stories are presented in the order of their publication, except the last two, which appear in the order they were written. "Reunion in Spain" (c.1962) also appears in chronological order but has not been previously published.

Contents

To Edward F. Dragon and Alfonso Ossorio,
encouraging and supportive friends
during most of the years
in which these stories were written.

Foreword

For writers, as for visual artists, the thought of a retrospective exhibition is threatening. In the art world, which moves more quickly than the literary world, a retrospective suggests a substantial body of completed work and therefore, a substantially completed life. For a living artist, the announcement of a retrospective may be a sort of premature death notice. It not only intimates mortality but anticipates the judgment of posterity. Each story (like each painting or sculpture) reveals a single moment in time and simultaneously transcends that particular moment, if only by its survival and reappearance. This ambiguity is further compounded by the difference between the author who worked, say forty or more years ago, and the one who is working now. They are different people and the same person. They have changed—perhaps developed, perhaps tired—and yet, to some extent, have remained consistent through the variety of these moments, as well as of places and moods. Finally, there is always the question of what's missing— the stories, in this instance, that have already gone out into the world in a previous collection or incorporated in novels, leaving only what art dealers call (especially if they're *buying*) "small works on paper."

Despite such reservations and anxieties, I hope that this collection, if not definitive, is representative and, if not comprehensive, is evocative of some moments worth commemorating in a retrospective.

B.H.F.

As I Am You Will Be

All the years of his young life Little Boy wanders the streets, looking at the beautiful girls and wanting them; all his young life he longs for the orgy that never comes. The conventions, the mores, the pressures of his group, bother him; never leave him free; they are to blame. The big experience never comes. Ecstasy is a word. Romance is paper and celluloid and Ernest Hemingway. He watches the truck drivers, the bartenders, the steve-dores, admiring their broad chests and narrow hips and their lives, their lives which pulse in the night. There is something about a strange face, a double shot of whiskey gulped down without a cough, tattooed arms.

Little Boy wanders, hating his clothes—the uni-form of his class—and envious of the men who don't wear ties.

The war comes—silently and secretly, like a worm eating an apple. At first he and his clique aren't bruised by the falling cards. But eighteen comes fast, fast enough so that Little Boy doesn't miss the big war. He may go marching off to camp with men, using all the strong words, hearing all about the big strong nights.

And Little Boy may get tattooed. Do you know what it is to walk into a tattooing parlor? Can you imagine choosing one label out of thousands as yours for life? Does the eagle seem to scream? Is the battleship too large? Is the Sailor's Grave too common? Is the seaman carrying a swab too cute? Would MOTHER, in capital letters, be flattered when she saw his arm? His eye finally lights upon a skull and crossbones with the motto: "As you are, I once was. As I am, you will be."

Little Boy rolls up his sleeve. Swede dry-shaves his arm and swabs it with alcohol. The stencil is applied and smeared with a black charcoal compound. Swede picks up the electric needle, dips it into heavy black ink, and follows the outline.

The boy holds fast on the left arm of the chair. Damp dead sweat trickles from under his arms. The needle works in and out on its course leaving blood in its wake and the boy grips the chair more tightly, thinking of the sea, and breaking with the parental yoke, and the blood and the needle, and in and out and in and out, and forever, which is a long time.

The needle looks caked and dirty. What about infection? What if some sailor before him had a disease? "Ya ain't a man till you've had a dose." "Blued, screwed, and tattooed." "Darling, don't forget your rubbers." Oh Boats, Oh Mate, Oh Mother, Oh God.

Swede finishes shading the central portion of the tattoo with a thicker needle which doesn't penetrate or hurt as much. He wipes the surface again with alcohol, but this time it bites and stings. Cool, soothing Vaseline and a gauze bandage.

"That'll stay on there good. Don't pick at it if it starts scabbing on ya."

The boy gives him three bucks and leaves.

For about two weeks the tattoo doesn't look just right. It is scabbed in spots and indistinct in others. And then it emerges—clean and sharp and part of you. You belong to a vast fraternity, encompassing all oceans and all ports, all roads and all jobs. When you walk into a bar in Shanghai, with your sleeves rolled up, you acquire a dozen friends. And a dozen men want to know you as you swim off the beach at Manila. The world is yours, the blood, the pulse, the ecstasy, the godhead you envisaged in a thousand strange thighs. No longer the prep-school frustration. You're a man of and among men. Forever, "As you are, I once was. As I am, you will be."

But the worm dies. It is the summer after the war. Seduction must replace purchase. "Intercourse," "sleeping with," "going to bed with," "oh shoot," all must be forced back into the vocabulary. And oh the polite cocktail parties and bridge games.

Forget that weekend in Frisco, when the water was running cold in the bathtub on a case of beer and four fifths of rye. Three sailors with their jumpers off played cut-throat pinochle for fourteen hours and a carton of Lucky Strikes—waiting for the knock on the door the pimply elevator boy had promised them. Making a four-hundred hand and waiting, waiting, waiting—until finally the knock. She'd take them all on for ten bucks. They cut, and his king was high. Christ, what a run of cards.

But now Susan bids four no-trump, and he knows she's using Blackwood, asking for aces, but he wants to ask the boys to beat a full-house.

"Five hearts."
"Five no."
"Six diamonds."
"Six spades."
"Pass."

"Pass."

"Pass."

He's dummy. He gets up and looks at his partner's hand. If the finesse doesn't work she'll go down—one trick—one dollar in Panama.

She makes her contract and tells him he bid nicely. Now they all want to go swimming, and the last one in is a monkey's uncle. So long ago he had drawn king high.

His tattoo is so-ooo cute, but really how could you? Were you drunk? God, you must have been really pickled. Cold sober? Early in the morning? In Norfolk? O priceless, priceless. Well, it really isn't so bad—I guess.

The cute little blonde, six years old, with curls bouncing on her shoulders, runs up to him.

"What's that, what's that?"

"It's a tattoo."

"What's a taboo?"

"Tattoo, tattoo. They make an indelible picture by pricking color into the skin."

What's indelible? Does it hurt? Does it hurt much?"

"Indelible means it never washes off. It didn't hurt much."

The president of his father's club sits down next to him in the hot room.

"You're Mike's son, aren't you?"

"Yes, sir."

"How'd you ever happen to get that?"

"I guess I was trying...I wasn't thinking very clearly...I was drunk."

He's in the shower room with his fraters for the first time:

"Ha ha. You salty dog. Why the hell did you ever get that thing? I almost got one; I'm damn glad I didn't.

A buddy of mine back home got tattooed, and his parents made him have it taken off. Has Susan seen it?"

He had dreamed of his return home and strutting across beaches and tiled floors flaunting his tattoo, but he found himself deliberately draping towels over his arm and buying long-sleeved sport shirts. Now, in the shower, he spreads the lather thickly on his arm.

The needle goes in and out, pricking beneath the skin. Superficially at least, he had always belonged to his group. He had all the right labels from the Roman numeral three after his name to the Hunt Club and Beach Club. What had happened? It would be different if he were a nigger, a wop, a Jew, but having a tattoo—that's such an unimportant thing.

Going to sleep, he made a tacit pact with God that if the tattoo was gone in the morning he would always believe in Him. A thousand times he looked expecting it to be gone. Finally, he made an appointment with a dermatologist.

Dr. Turner looks at the slip the nurse hands him and smiles.

"I assume since you're here you've made up your mind. It would be useless for me to try to dissuade you?"

"Yes, I've thought a lot about it, become self-conscious: I'd like it off."

"Well, let's take a look. Roll up your sleeve."

The doctor looks, pinching and stretching the skin, and remarking that the image is not really offensive. He calls for the nurse, and they lead the boy to the back room. Once again the surface is cleansed. The doctor keeps up a running commentary throughout the inquisition. He will try electrolysis, acid, and injections on parts of the tattoo. When the boy returns in two weeks, whichever method has shown the best results will be used to remove the entire thing.

The various treatments hurt about as much as the original tattooing, but in the sparks of the electrolysis needle he sees regained ease, and physical pain is of only secondary importance. Sore spots are covered by a bandage.

The two weeks go by suprisingly fast. He wonders which parts of the thing will be the first to go; a bone or an eye, a word or a phrase? He peeks under the bandage, sees three ugly little scabs.

He is early for his appointment. The doctor removes the bandage and with a scalpel scrapes away the scab. He shakes his head.

"I'm afraid it's in too deep, too deep. The only way to get it off is plastic surgery."

Charlie, the lifeguard, has a cruiser anchored on his chest. Joe, the locker boy at the gym, has five or six small tattoos all over his arms. What would they think of him? And what would his ex-mates think? Just before the end of he war, he used to talk a lot about what design he would get for the other arm.

"Would you make arrangements with the surgeon, please?"

The waiting room of the plastic surgeon is extremely crowded. Women with black eyes and bandaged noses sit looking at the words in fashion magazines. At last a big nurse with a little voice calls out the boy's name and he is ushered into the back office.

"I've arranged for an operating room at the hospital at two o'clock tomorrow. Will that be all right?"

"Fine."

"Good. Now let me see your arm."

The boy removes his coat and rolls up his sleeve.

"Not bad. Not bad. I was under the impression it was larger. That will come off nicely. We'll be able to use a local anaesthetic. You can watch the whole thing. Don't eat a heavy lunch, and turn in at the incoming patients' desk about half past one."

He signs his name at the desk and is turned over to an intern who hands him a white robe then prepares his arm for the operation. A sickening smell of ether pervades the place. NO SMOKING signs are everywhere. The minutes pass slowly. Promptly at two, the intern leads him into the operating room. There the surgeon waits, all in white except for the pink-tan rubber practicality of his hands, hands that represent the ultimate in social aesthetics. Those hands and a scalpel will make him feel comfortable on the beach and in the shower. They will deliver a scrap of flesh, a scrap of understanding and sensitivity, to the hospital sewage system , to the river, to its mother ocean. For a few days on beaches and in shower rooms laden with talcum powder he has known inferiority, but the pink-tan hands will cut this away. The left hand is smug, the right is complacent. The surgeon offers both, stretches them towards the boy.

The day before, the girl in the doctor's office with her new nose looked so relaxed, so completely untroubled and peaceful, almost animal. A bloodless operation. Black eyes and a swollen face for a few weeks. And then that wonderful freedom—freedom from feeling. The knife, cat-gut, anaesthesia offer this.

Cyrano, Cyrano. What a nose, what a man.

If the bullfrog had wings, he wouldn't bump his ass on the ground...If he were stronger...If the war...If society...If...

"Ready, nurse, the novocain."

Whisper

Can you hear me?

The New York I love is so cool you may not recognize her. Cooler than the neon at Times Square. Cooler than the drinks at Yankee Stadium. Cooler than the snow in Harlem. It's cool near the top.

I love what others hate: executive dining rooms of Wall Street banks, big legal offices with rows of CCH reports, the patterns made by teleregisters, and the way necktie stripes move up to the left among men who move to the right. The towers should be connected by bridges. I go down only to refuel—i.e., when not eating at some cloudy club. Down there, I like those filling stations in the mid-forties: Christ Cella, Pietro's, The Palm, and the French ones farther North. I like them because the food is good and cheaper than the places that cost money. New York is almost free, if you love your work. (Once I saw a guy ask a cab driver for a receipt.)

The skyline's free. I like leaving the city and returning to it by air. Robert Moses hasn't been able to organize the air. I like the top of the G.E. building, as visible from the garden behind our brownstone house, as are the chandeliers by Louis Comfort Tiffany in the windows of Third Avenue antique shops. I wish Comfort were my middle name.

I'm too well dressed to go into Third Avenue bars; my clothes are always picking fights with people. Are my lapels as narrow as piping? I miss the protective shadows of the el.

The guys are right who look in garbage cans, *if they don't have to*. They're painters or poets or businessmen. I like everything disposable. Cigarettes, whiskey, newspapers, soap, candy bars, razor blades—those are the businesses to be in. Imagine going to bed each night with the knowledge that you have packaged people's desires, that you have given them that sense of reality only waste can give. I like art before it goes into museums. I like a city that can throw away the Ritz without batting an eye (and then sell its elevator cabs to Texas oilmen to convert into ranch-style bars). I like what's in parentheses, too, more than seeing those same cabs sold to Hollywood as lampbases. If life is a choice between lampbases and bookends, I choose bookends because they remind me of parentheses. If life is a choice...

I like the papers I see on businessmen's desks: Dun & Bradstreet reports ("Credit Is Man's Confidence In Man"), Proudfoot, Dodge, Standard and Poor's, Moody's. Moody I like best of all. I wish Moody were my last name. I picture him as he must have been: a beard. The others all sound as though they knew exactly what they were doing. I like letterheads, trademarks, logotypes. I like statements of profit and loss. I like black ink. I like analyses of projected income, inventories, contracts, licenses, permits, legal documents of all kinds but preferably those in pale blue binders. Getting and spending we lay waste our money. I like the printed literature that comes from trade associations. I don't forget that it wasn't always printed. I don't forget the tender New York girls who took it down in Pitman or Gregg. Take me down gently, gently, as you would a word. I like the sad world of the wastepaper basket. I like the cleaning ladies who give office buildings that arbitrarily illuminated look at night. Seagram is wrong. Uniform elegance is wrong. Waste can't be that well organized. Oh, that blue light, again, at the top of the G.E. building. I wish Comfort were my middle name. I wish I had a first name, instead of initials.

What else goes on at night besides the lights? The music. You've got to be crazy to pass a law forbidding people to blow their horns. I hate low quiet cities. I like it up high where the hum bounces between Rockefeller Center and Wall Street. I like, too, those sterling phoenixes of the boom, the Empire State and Chrysler buildings. (I like to think that the latter was named for a violinist who hit high notes.) I like thin air. I make exceptions sometimes of the Village Vanguard or Birdland. I usually regret it. Hell went underground in the fifties (like everyone was digging like). I like places where you walk straight in: Five Spot, Jazz Gallery, Half Note, if you can get a cab to go to Hudson Street. I like Hudson. I like his river. The big ones with the Indian names all belong to Thomas Wolfe. This river belongs to us. A crazy river with nothing but a destination. It's just kind of there to say hello to, like Santa Claus outside of Macy's at Christmas. The East River's crazy too. It's just kind of there to say hello to, like Santa Claus outside of Blomingdale's at Christmas.

New York has two seasons now, according to the engineers. There's that foggy time during the summer that makes me want to try *haiku:*

> *Moon rain*
> *air-conditions*
> *New York streets*

Or:

> *New York*
> *moon rain*
> *from air-conditioners*

Or:

> *Air-conditioners*
> *moon rain*
> *New York*

and there's that steamy time in winter, when the verse forms become complicated and you can't get tickets to anything, and the stores, even the little ones upstairs, are crowded.   Smoking a cigar after lunch, I watch the executives ice-skating; they wear pin-striped suits and scarves and gloves. New York is a Japanese Egyptian etcetera kind of place. All the different newspapers and magazines at Hotalings. All the different kinds of cars in the automobile showrooms. When are the Russians going to build a good sports car? I want to drive a fast car to the moon. I want to touch the real moon rain.

I like the invisible voices, the frequency-modulated voices: Jean Shepherd, William B. Williams, and now Mort Fega. I like the idea that people who sleep during the day can get the commercials at night.

There's nothing on Broadway except a few good movies that will reach your neighborhood playhouse. (My neighborhood playhouse is my bed; my living room is my bedroom; the TV's so close I can touch it.) There's not much off Broadway either. The best plays are being made in bed—or never get produced. I hate the whole theatre-concert-prison situation. I want to drink and smoke and move around. The best thing about theater is the intermission. I like the furs and cigarette holders. I like that particular draft which enters lobbies in the West Forties. J like the dash to the nearest bar. I like the Rolls with the blue lamp up on top.

I like the hearses that even the cabbies respect. I hope I leave town tying up traffic, on my way to suburbs so full of cemeteries they can bury everybody horizontally even though the efficiency experts recommend vertically.

Efficiency experts! Experts of all kinds! Business is a world of delights I cannot afford in the other world, the world of home. This is my home, my recaptured childhood, where chairs swivel and roll around on little wheels, where I have two telephones on my desk, where the drawers slide out on runners (never too far), where the bar in the executive conference room has an executive refrigerator with an executive ice tray in which there's always enough executive ice, etc. I have a secretary who frees me for business and from bills, personal income tax forms, wife presents, dealings with garage mechanics, watch repairmen, G.E. (in the other home everything breaks). Just a phone call for shirts or underwear or socks: always the same. She can buy my anonymity from haberdashers as others buy their identity. My identity is my anonymity. I don't exist anywhere away from my office, except in other people's offices. I adore this girl who understands the subtleties of a *Who's Who* questionnaire, who understands a thousand subtleties I can't understand. "Put Mr. A. on. Mr. B. is waiting." I'm Mr. B. I'm not waiting.

There are messengers waiting to be shot in any direction. And there's a supply closet—toy closet, I almost said—full of rubberbands and clips and rulers and staples and machines for writing (the French call them) and machines for adding and machines for dictating and machines for duplicating luxuries, like nonsmudge carbon paper. At home, what have I to compare with these? What have I to fill the time? A wife, children, a house. Nothing. At home I have myself. Evenings, holidays, weekends, I must manufacture the irritations that are mine, free, at the office. At home there's always the possibility that the decision may be important. At business, the important thing is to decide.

I have decided, like a certain kind of artist (the artist as businessman), to bet on the future. Contrary to popular belief (my secretary's phrase—I adore her, I adore her), New York doesn't exist in the present. It doesn't exist. It is becoming. It is the future. It is aims, plans, preconceptions, projects, ends. It is my city, the city of tomorrow's sale. I'll find myself here. There's no time now, but I have forever. I'll find myself, somewhere, out there. (I say this, looking straight ahead into the windows of another office. I'm afraid to look down.)

It is fitting that Mr. Moses is our Commissioner. He digs the future. He hates us. He hates now. But he likes World's Fairs. He sees the future in statistics, traffic and population trends. We're nothing. We're the six or seven zeros.

Nothing is everything. I don't want the adventures of a sailor. I don't want the space of a flyer. I don't want the strength of an athlete. I don't want the dreams of an artist. If I wanted them I'd buzz my secretary. Money talks quietly, like me. It's all zeros. Duels, now, are fought with zeros. The best tables are bought with zeros. The best seats are bought with zeros. Money whispers. Bills never crackle in the hands of a headwaiter or a cop. Power used to be noisy. Not now. Now type-writers are silent. Now carpets are thick. Now acoustical tile (simulating travertine) soaks up sound everywhere. And even in the general offices vinyl has replaced as-phalt; it's quieter, and easier on the feet of clerks who wear sponge-rubber soles so thick one hardly hears them take their coffee breaks. For them the day is all soft silent foods, a mush of doughnuts and coffee mid-morning and mid-afternoon. At lunch they have hamburgers and ice cream, while I chew glass. They're not yet rich enough to chew.

Zeros! And less than zeros: minus quantities. Deductions. Everything's deductible. I'm deductible. Cocteau, I think it was, remarked that for the poet $2 + 2 = 5$. For the institution $2 + 2 = 3$. There seem to be twelve men siting around the conference table. There are only nine; three got lost, ground up among the cigar butts. Everyone has a hand on the wheel of the steering com-mittee. It can't move. Sub-sub-sub-sub a committee down to one, and there's hope. Two minds are worse than one. The institution is always equal to less than the sum of its parts, and those parts are always equal to less than the sum of their parts. What's good for General Motors (or Electric or Aniline or Telephone) is lousy for me. I'm better than my corporate identity. I'm better than the exact fraction I represent of my club, staff, nation, bu-reau, organization, etc. I'm better in indirect proportion to the number of people who shape me in a given situation. I'm better anonymous. I'm better as nothing. I'm better as zero than minus one.

    It's quiet. The whisper you hear is air rushing through sheet-metal ducts, hissing its snakesong, forever, 72°F., 50% relative humidity. The air is filtered. The seasons are filtered. The engineers are wrong. There's one season.

    No summer reading for me. What do I read, away from the office? It doesn't matter much; everything's important. Anything that fits in my pocket. Anything that will replace the ringing of the phone: IRRITANTS. At LaGuardia I pick up Shattuck's *The Banquet Years*, a reprint, of course; I'm always a few years behind. My wife and my secretary read the current books for me (just as they see the new movies and I watch the old ones on TV). I read about yesterday. Doing that makes New York possible. Thesis: tomorrow. Antithesis: yesterday. Synthesis: now, an illusion. *The Banquet Years*, about the birth of the avant-garde before the avant-garde went into business. Hell, three big banquets in thirty years (for Rousseau, Apollinaire, and Saint-Pol-Roux)! I'm invited to three a week at grand ballrooms, one grander than the next. Was fun half as much fun before it became business? Shattuck says near the end: "The most notable artistic figures of the Banquet Years practiced external non-conformity in order to attain a conformity within the individual." I practice external conformity in order to attain a non-conformity within myself. If tension builds I turn it into words. Better than letting it turn into ulcers or cancer.

    Everything works. Nothing is wasted. Would it have made any difference if rather than Shattuck, I had read Bonnie Golightly's latest, or *The Persian Wars?* All I want is for the phone to keep ringing and the air to rush through its ducts. Odd, the shock sometimes when, precisely at six, it stops. Like any businessman, it's at times like these (evenings,weekends), I find my theme: (Journal entry, 10/23/60) *It is Sunday. My wife and son have gone to Long Island for the day. I am left with silence. The silence is my leisure. I don't know what to do with it. I listen. I hear it, the silence, rushing by like air, like the air in air-conditioning ducts. There is no balance to the silence, no calm, no poise—only pressure. This silence, this luxury, this leisure begs insistently to be enjoyed—and destroyed. Finally, I scream. For a few seconds, during the scream, it is quiet, and then the noise begins again.*

Appreciate whispers. Two cars collide at an intersection. It's a beautiful sound, but what does it mean?

But the fifties were my season in heaven. Here the best paintings were made, and music played. Here you could get a copy of *Adolphe* at Walgreen's and find no place to hide among the columns under Lever House. Everything was happening. If only the critics had been driven out of town, tarred and feathered with copies of *Art News*. Nobody listened to Barney Newman: "Aesthetics is for the artists like ornithology is for the birds."

The sixties will be greater yet. Up, up into the highest cholesterol. Up, up into the highest brow. Fat will be fashionable. Baldness will be fashionable. The moon will continue to be fashionable. There'll be souped-up elevators in office buildings. There'll be souped up office buildings in outer space. All soups will be cool and chic: gazpacho, vichysoisse, infinity. Everyone will have his bowl of infinity. There'll be second helpings of infinity.

Just tell the waiter, quietly, you want more. The coolness of it all. The endless whispers of it all send endless shivers up my endless spine. Up, up to the ears. I can hardly hear me.

Reunion in Spain

There was always tension between Max Kraus and me. Always, ever since the mid-'fifties, when he was beginning to show his paintings and I was beginning to publish frequently in the art magazines. So there was that—from his viewpoint, anyway—artist versus critic. That and its only slightly less abstract ramifications—the struggling artist versus the increasingly successful, presumably unstruggling journalist; passionate paint versus clinical criticism; and yes, oh yes, man versus woman.

Starting with the first group show in which Max appeared, I singled out his work, tried to explain it, to translate it into words. He responded with a note:

> Dear Enid Sloan,
> Thanks for your seemingly sympathetic words. But my work's not about "whiplash line" or "frontal attack." And it's not about "shallow space" or "holding the picture plane," either. It's about paint—paint's color, thickness, juiciness.
> Max Kraus

This led to our meeting. He was a few years older than me, somewhere in his early forties, but he seemed still older, more worn. I could see that the furrows in his brow would become permanent. His beard, almost blond, already looked gray. Only his eyes were young. Their bright blue gaze darted from my mouth to the space above my head, as if following each disappearing word to some distant destination.

"Your note wasn't very gracious," I began. "All I do, all I try to do, is clarify the artist's intent —"

"Clarify! Is that what you call it? Well, you're the writer. But I can think of other words—*oversimplify, approximate.*"

"Gracious as ever."

"Stop all this garbage about graciousness. I thought you were interested in my work. My note was meant to be helpful."

"So was my review."

"It was. In a way. On the career level. I just wanted you to understand, what *I* do isn't important—my stance, my gesture—I don't think about those things. What's important is what *paint* does. That's what I think about. The rest embarrasses me."

More words from him led to more articles by me. But, judging by Max's reactions, nothing I wrote could ever be more than approximate or less than embarrassing, not even my long laudatory review of his first one-man show. Still, largely because of it, other critics visited his studio, collectors and curators followed, and his work began to sell.

I suppose Max was grateful to me, ambivalently grateful, his kind of grateful. Anyway, I didn't expect thanks, didn't expect anything. I was surprised when his present arrived—a canvas, maybe three feet by four, carefully wrapped. I put it face down on the floor, cut the packing tape and heavy paper, and before turning it

over, came to the inscription scrawled in black magic-
marker:

> To Enid,
> who believes that art
> like any commodity,
> must be wrapped in words.
> From Max,
> who believes that words
> should be wrapped in art.

I found the message condescending, chillingly sardonic,
labored too. Max had worked on it—I knew that.

On the other side of the canvas was a strong
composition, mostly in black, with scraps of paper col-
laged beneath the heavy paint. As usual I admired Max's
energy and his control of what he'd called paint's "juici-
ness," now playing against freely torn edges of paper. It
took a few minutes of close looking to realize that the
scraps were torn from my reviews of his work.

I thought of returning his gift but didn't because
I really like it, liked it as art if not as message. Instead, I
put it in my storage closet and looked at it only two or
three times during the next couple of months. Each time
I liked it better, and each time, besides reminding me of
Max, it reminded me to try, in my work, to wrap my
words in art. During this period I didn't see Max and I
didn't call him, although at one of the openings he
should have been at I heard that he and his third wife had
separated. That made it more difficult for me to call,
more obvious. I waited, continued to peek at the painting
occasionally, and finally hung it.

After another month or so he called. "I guess you
didn't like it. Or, knowing how gracious *you* are, maybe
you didn't get it?"

"I got it, all right. I like some things about it—particularly the paint."

He laughed. "It's a good work. Hang onto it. It'll be worth a fortune someday. Look, I've been going through a difficult divorce. It's settled now, and I'm off to Spain. Just wanted to say good-bye. Thought maybe if you're going to be in Europe you might come to see me—me and my work. It always explodes when I'm in a new place."

"You talk as if Spain's down the block. I don't expect to be there. But write if you have a chance. Let me know just where you are."

His first letter, from a town on the outskirts of Barcelona, contained a dozen Polaroids of new work. "I've always vacillated," he wrote, "between tight art in a loose environment and loose art in a tight environment. Here I tend toward the latter. My fantasy is order."

I smiled as I read these words from dear orderly Max. Max, whose third marriage had just gone kaput. Max, whose children, I'd heard, were scattered from coast to coast. Max, who had given up his studio and left New York just as he was beginning to have some success here. Max, who was, in brief, wrecking his barely middle-aged life and blossoming career...I stopped short, turning to my own life, my own career. The few discreet affairs, without the mess of marriage and children and divorce. The steady output of article after article, until there were enough now for a coming collection. The commissions to do catalogue introductions and monographs. The projects being planned for still more books. All of this was *order*, each effort stable as stone, each stone in place.... And yet there was a singleness of purpose in his life as in his work, a direction that cut through his

career to the work itself. He worked regardless of everything. I worked because of everything. He shaped chaos.
Chaos—the details of life—shaped me.

I tried to explain all of this in my reply: "Your
fantasy is order. Mine is disorder. We nourish each
other's fantasies. My days are all appointments and
deadlines. I accept more jobs than I want—" As I typed,
I recognized belatedly how much Max's style was influ-
encing mine. In everything he said or wrote, as in everything he painted, there was a clarity and, yes, an *order-
liness* that I envied. But I didn't write that to him. Instead,
I finished by saying, "I envy your being in Spain."

"Geography is internal..." his next letter began.
And so it went, back and forth, in a relationship that
became closer in correspondence than it had been in
person. Our needs were answered at long distance. In
New York neither of us would have devoted the necessary time to each other precisely when it was wanted. By
mail, we didn't have to—we were able to choose the time
with absolute freedom.

The letters became gradually more affectionate
and playful. Max wrote that I was in complete control of
my control. I wrote back that he was in complete control
of his lack of control. His reality spoke across the sea to
my fantasy, my reality to his fantasy. I looked forward to
his letters as he must have to mine. We wrote to each
other more and more frequently, often now on impulse
rather than as obligatory reply. Max sent postcards too—
a flurry of terse messages, some in Spanish, and images
ranging from flamenco dancers to bullfighters, from
Velázquez to Tapiès, from the Alhambra to Gaudi's Sa-
grada Familia. Often I found myself needing a Spanish-
English dictionary. Even more often I wondered who

was with him at museums and mosques, at bullfights and cafes. Who shared his *vino*, his *casa*, his *cama*? Could I believe the letters and cards, in which he was always alone, always asking when I'd visit?

When? When would I ever be able to squeeze a trip into my schedule? As I ground out article after article, introduction after introduction, I sometimes took amphetamines to help me meet deadlines. Then, only then, usually late at night, exhausted but unable to sleep, I'd speed to Spain, bringing Max my words, my world. My east-fifties brownstone, as brown as Iberian mud. My floor-through—and through and through, as my mind raced back and forth from one end of the apartment to the other. My walls covered with art including his, as black as Goya's blackest paintings. My radiator pounding like clogs and castanets... Words flew from my mind to my fingers and from there through the air to Max.

"You're losing your critical detachment," he wrote. "I know what's going to happen next. You'll become dissatisfied with the approximate quality of words. You'll want to paint. It always happens—every time I think a relationship is going well the woman decides to paint."

Max was being silly—I've never had any desire to paint—but, beyond that, the word "relationship" struck me. It seemed "approximate," suggesting something much more complete than what actually existed between us. In fact, it suggested what *should* have existed.

I determined to make the approximate truly proximate. I turned down several projects. I wrote and wrote, trying to catch up on assignments already accepted. I was almost with Max, part of the crowd in the bullring, when he wrote that he would be returning to New York. It was understood he would stay with me until he found a studio.

Max took over. Portfolios, rolled canvases, cartons of paint and brushes were piled in the living room. His clothes, toilet articles, beer bottles were everywhere. The phone became his. He made dozens of calls, spreading the word about his need for a studio. One painter was going to teach on the West Coast, another was leaving for Rome on a fellowship, still another was leaving for Paris, but none of their studios was right. Each had a problem—the location, the space itself, the light.

I was relieved. I liked having Max where he was. We had made love the night he arrived. That was my trip to Spain—that and the flamenco records he played and the bullfight passes he taught me with a pillow case and the guidebooks he explained, pointing to a particular detail of the mosque in Cordova or of a painting by Hieronymous Bosch, whom he now called "El Bosco." I wrote little, adapting myself to his hours, drinking beer with him, seeing his friends.

For a few weeks, no matter how disconnected from the realities of work and time, we shared an openness that was, of course, much more exposed that what can exist in any correspondence. I don't mean only our sexual contact or our constant physical proximity and sharing of possessions, but our immediate responses, spontaneous gestures, things that can't be put on paper. Our life, our *relationship* during this brief period seemed to exist without censorship, without editing. And then, as suddenly as Max had appeared, he began to disappear—always in the afternoon, always at the same hour, always with the excuse of "a professional appointment." He refused further explanation. The door closed on openness.

Well, he had his secrets, and I had mine—the festering suspicion and jealousy that distracted me from writing, especially during the afternoon, which should now have been my most productive period of work. *Should have been*, if Max didn't loom over my desk in dozens of erotic positions with the female partners of his so-called professional appointments—predatory art dealers, young painters eager to take instruction, collectors on the prowl for new talent (certified by me!). I tried to keep busy. Once again I accepted too many assignments. Once again I began using amphetamines. But now I wasn't using them only to meet my deadlines—even more I wanted to relieve the depression caused by my jealousy. I wanted to be high and peppy for Max when he returned from his appointments.

In reserve, at the back of my desk drawer, I also had some pills a friend at an art magazine had given me. "It's called Hubrisine," she'd said. "A new psychedelic. Sensual and spiritual all at once. Take it with someone you love. Save it for the right moment."

The moment came one evening when Max was particularly late. He'd said he would stop at an opening after his appointment and that he might not return until six-thirty or seven. It was eight. I took a tablet of Hubrisine, washed it down with beer, put a flamenco record on the player, and waited for Max.

Soon I was in Spain with him. Max wearing those high tight pants, stamping his boots on the floor precisely and assertively. Me moving toward him, hands over head, clicking castanets, one bare shoulder forward, then the other, back arched, torso beckoning... Everything was clear, composed, balanced. Max and I belonged together. No other woman could give him what I could give, had given, would continue to give.

The room throbbed. The carpet was alive, an exotic weave of growing grass. I kicked off my slippers and walked carefully to the record player —very carefully so as not to crush the grass—and turned down the volume. The music continued to pound, as if picture hooks were being hammered into a neighboring wall. Suddenly, sunshine poured through the wall and I could see a landscape hanging there filled with Seville oranges so bright I winced. Shutting my eyes, I stumbled to the mirror. My pupils were enlarged, still enlarging—two dark mouths opening to swallow my face. I gulped more beer. Its bubbles were as sharp as Toledo steel.

Where was Max? Sipping gazpacho or sangria somewhere? Extending his appointment beyond the opening, beyond me, beyond time? The very idea of time made me laugh There was so much of it. I could feel it — hours, days, weeks, months, years—dripping from the walls, oozing across the floor, watering the carpet. There was forever.

Almost forever. Forever interrupted now, finally, by the crash of Max's key in the door. The roar of tumblers falling, knob turning. The shriek of hinges. The explosion of the door slamming shut. The slow squeak of shoe leather moving through grass.

"Hi, Enid."

"Oh, yes. Very." My voice sounded as distant, as unrecognizable, as his.

"What've you been up to?"

"Exactly. My question exactly."

I felt the shagginess of his beard against my cheek, as he said, "You sound edgy."

"No, just thinking about you, you and your appointments. Tell me about them."

"Not now. You'll see. Enough to say I'm doing what I've always done—making order out of chaos."

"Not enough! Not enough to say."

He looked at me, silvery golden beard fluttering. I started to count the gray hairs in it. I was up to eleven when he asked, "What d'you want, for God's sake? I was going to surprise you." He paused dramatically. "It's two months since I left Barcelona."

"That's no surprise. Sorry you left?"

"No, sorry I'm not painting. I got off to a fast start there—you remember the Polaroids—but then I slowed down, began looking at art instead of making it. I've been looking ever since, wondering what I can ever do, compared with Velázquez, Goya —"

"Don't compare. It's a waste of energy. You were doing fine."

"*Were*. My doctor thinks —"

Max's words reached me as slowly as he had crossed the room. "Your doctor?"

"I was going to him before I left, paying him in paintings. He didn't like the idea of my trip, and he doesn't like what I'm doing now. Thinks there's nothing wrong with the studios I've seen. Thinks I'm stalling. Thinks I want to stay here with you."

"You can do both—paint, get a studio somewhere, even a small one, and stay with me."

The room was aglow again with oranges and crimson capes, athrob with guitars and castanets. I wanted to share all this—the good part of Hubrisine—with Max. I offered him a pill.

"I'm sensitive to drugs."

His words hung in the air like small pockets of pain, wounds, stigmata. I realized that his saying this was as hard for him as telling me that he was back in therapy.

"Then maybe you shouldn't."

"Don't treat me like a cripple!"

"That's a bit strong. I *understand* that artists are sensitive. It's my profession—*understanding* that, *explaining* how you make order out of chaos."

"Worse! —the condescending critic, the sarcastic scribe."

"What colorful labels. But you'll paint them black, won't you?"

He paced for a moment, then poured himself a beer. I thought that was that, that the psychedelic voyage I'd planned for the two of us was over, that I'd complete it alone. For a change he'd play critic and watch while I played artist, painting pictures in my mind, strumming and slapping a guitar, choosing one medium after another or letting each choose me, play me....I was surprised when Max snatched the pill and washed it down.

For a long time we sat listening to the music without talking. He was the first to speak.

"Cold, this world of yours," he said. "You're wearing a sweater. I need one too."

He walked to the bedroom very slowly, as if fighting his way through a blizzard, then returned in a rough oily fisherman's cardigan, rubbing his hands together and blowing on them.

"And bright," he added. "Cold and bright."

I looked at him standing in front of a wall of shivering books. "You left the light on in the bedroom."

"Please don't do that, either. You're not my mother. Just my critic." He flicked the bedroom switch. "Did you see that? When I turned off the bedroom light, the lamps in here became brighter."

I laughed. I couldn't stop laughing, even as I watched Max's blood rush from beneath his face to its hairy surface. For a moment I thought he was wearing a deep red mask. Then I thought just the opposite: that he had removed his usual mask of skin.

"I make a simple observation and you laugh."

"I'm not laughing at you, Max. You've probably discovered a physical law: the current that couldn't get into the bedroom light rushed to the lamps in here. Is that what you meant?"

"We'll see. We'll see what happens with this. "He turned off the player. "I *know*. You're always a step ahead of me. But what you *don't know* is what's happening in *other* apartments. The sound had to go somewhere. It's *real*."

His mask was getting redder. "It's real," I replied very quietly as I mashed out a cigarette.

Max crouched over it. "That too. It's so real, as real as a cigarette butt with lipstick on it. It is *really* a cigarette butt with lipstick on it. But once you point out anything, it becomes less real."

He rose from his crouching position and pointed at me. "For example —" he began, still pointing. Again, I laughed. "Typical! Everything becomes little humorous notes for your articles. They'll become the reality. Suppose they *are* reality. What then? I'm clutching at reality, and I've got nothing to hang onto but your criticism." Max laughed now. "You understand, Enid, none of this is personal. I like your writing, but if *it* is reality, where's *my* reality? I'm going to keep quiet for a while. Am I talking too much? Is it all right?"

"If you want to talk, talk."

"Well, there's no such thing as constructive criticism, I know that. It's like laughter, constructive laughter—it's too abstract. And if you laugh when there's nothing to laugh at, it's an affectation."

"Is that constructive criticism?"

"I don't know. I'm going to find out." Max went into the bedroom, switched on the light, and reappeared in the doorway a moment later. "Just go on talking as if I weren't here." He was gone again, then back again. "I wanted to look at some of my Barcelona paintings. They're full of sunshine. They make me feel warm." He returned to the bedroom, stayed there another moment, then stood again in the doorway. "It's amazing the way one can step into and out of reality. But which room is reality? Those paintings are mushy. I can't go in there again. It's too real."

Max held onto the doorjambs, steadying himself, then slid slowly to the floor, and began sobbing. For a split second I thought he was acting. I felt the laughter swelling inside me again—a nervous reflex or maybe an affectation, as Max had said—and then it stopped, at my heart. I could feel the collision there, that specifically—the laughter and my heart, pounding at each other—as, between sobs, Max began speaking.

"What about crying?" he asked from the floor. "Is that all right?"

"Anything."

"Good old Enid, the voice of reality, the written voice of reality. I see through you. Literally, I see through you. I see the books behind you. I see the pictures behind you. I see everything that's behind you. You must find it odd that there's nothing behind me."

Max was almost on his knees as I rushed to help him stand. When I reached him, he lurched past me toward a small red painting on the wall.

"We're all in the same boat," he said, looking at this work by another artist. "It was so real, I really thought it was *something*. Blood. But it's *nothing*. Just paint. Can you hear me, Enid? Are you here? The story of my life. Asking that. Are you here? Say something, Enid. Tell me you're here."

"I'm here, Max."

"Keep talking." At the bedroom doorway, he stopped, with one foot raised, in the middle of a step. "I can't get through."

"Maybe just as well."

"No!" He sank to the floor and started crying again. "The carpet's real and the floor beneath it's real. Everything's real except me. I have to talk to someone who hasn't take this drug." He pushed hard against the floor and rose in a direct ascending line to the phone on the coffee table. "Busy," he announced after a long wait, then tried again. "Still busy."

"Let me help."

Max slowly recited a number that began like a series of coincidences. The exchange was the same as mine. The next digit was too. And the next. And the next. And, finally, the last. I laughed. "This number! No wonder it's busy."

"I was trying to reach my doctor. I've got to talk to someone from the world of reality." He went to the window and looked out. "There are people out there from the other world. I can't stand this."

"Sorry. I feel responsible. I've had similar experiences. I didn't take them so seriously. As you've noticed,

I laugh. I laugh knowing that the pain will go away. Even madness —"

"Don't say it. I've—got—to—talk—to—some-one—from—the —real—world." The staccato words were surrounded by silence. "I've—got—to—talk—to—Doctor—Rose. Doctor—Eli—Rose."

I called information. The operator gave me a number. I repeated it to Max. "Sound right?"

"Doctor—Eli—Rose. Doctor—Eli—Rose."

I dialed the number and got an answering service. "This is Enid Sloan. I'm a friend of Max Kraus—a patient of Dr. Rose's. Mr. Kraus is anxious to speak to the doctor. My number is—"

"Tell him it's an emergency"

"It's an emergency, " I repeated before giving my number.

"You reached him?"

"His service."

"When's he coming?"

"I don't know."

"Tell him it's an emergency."

"I did."

"Then call again."

"I don't want to tie up the line."

We sat, looking at the phone, waiting for it to ring.

"It's so real," Max said, "almost as real as a phone that rings." He paused. "I had a phone once that didn't ring. D'you know why? Because I had it cut off. Didn't want anyone disturbing me in my studio. That's what I thought. Dr. Rose thought just the opposite. He said I was afraid that no one *would* call, that no one *would* disturb me. "They're subtle, these shrinks, but not as subtle as silent phones."

"That's better."

"What is?"

"Your mood. Maybe when Dr. Rose calls, we'll just let the phone ring."

"How can we let it ring when it's not ringing?"

Finally it rang. Max reached toward the phone, then dropped his hand. " Fill him in, Enid. Please—"

"I'm a friend of Max's," I began, as Max watched me, listening to every word. "He's here. We took a drug called Hubrisine... H-U-B-R-I-S-I-N-E... A psychedelic, I think.. We each took one. I took mine earlier, maybe three hours ago... I don't know anything about its legality... Why! For pleasure, for relief... There's no point in this. I'll put Max on."

As Max spoke, I became more and more resentful of the doctor's inquisition. Yes, I had offered the pill, but I'd also said that maybe Max shouldn't take it. Yes, I felt partly responsible, but Max was the one who'd grabbed it.

"Everything's so real," I heard Max saying. "Light. Sound. Cigarettes. The walls. The floor... Yes... The Emergency Ward... Yes... He wants to speak to you, Enid."

"You don't want to go there."

"He says if you don't get on the phone, he'll send the police."

Max leaned on me as we walked to Second Avenue to get a southbound cab. There was an illuminated phone booth on the corner.

"Call Dr. Rose," Max said once again.

"You've changed your mind?" I asked hopefully.

"You've changed my mind, " Max snarled. "With that stuff you gave me."

"For God's sake, Max don't you start this. Your shrink's bad enough. If you're feeling better, I could call and say you'll see him at the usual time tomorrow. You don't belong in the hospital. You don't need to go along with his power plays."

"He said to get me to the hospital. I've got to go someplace real."

I hailed a cab. As soon as I'd given the driver the address, I turned to Max. "Are you sure you want this? I can tell him to turn around and take us home."

"Dr. Eli Rose... Dr. Eli Rose..." Max droned on, staring straight ahead.

A young doctor in a white coat was at the entrance to the emergency ward. "Kraus?" For a moment I thought he was greeting a chronic patient. "Dr. Rose phoned," he continued, as he led us into the white-tiled receiving room. "He's given us the pertinent information." He glanced at a form on his clipboard, then at Max. "I understand you've taken a drug called Hubrisine?" He waited. Max said nothing, did nothing, just stared straight ahead as he had in the cab. For the first time the doctor looked directly at me. I nodded, and he looked at the form.

"Edith Sloan?"

"Enid."

"What's your relationship to the patient?"

The doctor smiled. Max smiled.

"My *friend* gave me this pill. It was real. In an unreal way. And now I need something. The other pill. The *real* pill. In a *real* way."

"We don't know anything about what you took. It's not in any of the books."

"It's new," I said. "Can't you just give him a sedative?"

"That may be contra-indicated. The best we can do is let him sleep it off and hope there's no permanent damage."

"He can do that at my apartment."

"I'll call Dr. Rose."

"Call Dr. Rose," Max echoed him. "I know I'm creating this hallucination. I know it. But that doesn't make it less real. This place looks like a hospital. It smells like a hospital."

I squeezed Max's hand. "We're at the hospital. It's real."

As I spoke, a boy in black jeans and a leather jacket covered with cut-glass bike buttons moved across the room toward a uniformed nurse standing at a sterilizer. He carried one arm inside his jacket as if reaching for a weapon. His sparkling darkness loomed more and more threateningly as the nurse seemed to disappear into the shiny white walls.

"Listen, Honey, I been waiting. I gotta get outta here."

"Don't call me Honey."

"Okay, Honey, but—"

She spun around with a pair of hot forceps in her hand. "Don't call me that again. Just wait your turn."

"I been waiting. I been watching them go ahead of me." He pointed at Max and me. "*They* look okay. I got a busted hand—Honey."

She waved the forceps in his face. "We all got problems. I've been on my feet all night. I'm working. What did you do to get here? You sure as hell weren't working."

"Was *they* working?" he asked, pointing at Max and me.

A policeman entered the waiting room. I didn't know at first if he was there to help the nurse or to arrest me. He led the boy to a bench at the far end of the room, then held the door open for two orderlies wheeling a stretcher. The boy's hand would finally be attended to, I thought, but the orderlies went right past him to Max. I watched them and the doctor talking to him. I watched him climb onto the stretcher. I watched him being strapped to it with strips of canvas. I watched them park him opposite a large fluoroscopic screen. Max was so willing, so docile, that he seemed unreal, un-Max. I had the feeling that this quiet drama, this gray shadow-play on the white wall was meant to contrast with the more violent black -and- white vignette performed by the boy and the nurse.

"My hand's killing me!" the boy screamed. "You gotta do something."

The nurse called a doctor, another invisible figure in white. He placed the boy's hand on the fluoroscope. Suddenly the bones of his hand and wrist were suspended in space on the screen facing Max. I saw Max stir and moved closer to him, trying to block his view.

"I know I'm creating my own hallucination," Max whispered. "That's a real drug. You gave me a real drug." He lowered his voice still more. "As long as you're wearing that sweater and I'm wearing this one, everything's okay. They're my last hold on reality. For God's sake, don't take it off."

The young doctor returned. "I reached Dr. Rose. He wants Kraus put under observation."

"See?" Max said. "What you thought was a hand is really an eye. An eye disguised as a hand watching me watching you watching me."

A woman I hadn't seen come into the receiving room pulled at my sleeve. "Don't let them keep him here. They'll put him into some cell and let him rot. That's what they mean by observation. Run for it while you've got the chance." I pointed at Max. "I'll help you. We can smuggle him out."

The doctor stepped between the woman and me. "We're going to transfer Kraus to Psychiatric." He motioned to the orderlies. "Best for you to stay with him during the transition."

The transition from what to what? From fantasy to reality? From reality to fantasy? I remembered how Max had looked popping in and out of my bedroom doorway. Then he was still on his feet; now he was strapped to a stretcher. As I followed him into the elevator, the woman blew us a kiss.

The elevator descended to a dimly lit tunnel of stone and concrete. I stayed alongside Max, walking fast to keep up with the orderlies. There was no sound except for their footsteps and the click of my heels and the whir of the stretcher's wheels, all echoing in the passage like the flamenco music Max had turned off and sent somewhere else—here. As if by agreement, no one had anything to say in this subway without tracks, without trains, without platforms, without passengers.

Max seldom opened his eyes. When he did, he looked at me without expression and then shut them again. Perhaps he was reassured by me. More likely he was frightened by the seeming endlessness of this line, this express route from Emergency to Psychiatric. I didn't want to think about the stations that lay beyond—Cardiac, Cancer—terminal stops on the ultimate ride.

"I know I'm hallucinating," Max told me as we entered another elevator.

"We're going to a different ward."

"Don't say it."

"Say what?"

"What you were about to say. About what I'm doing, where I'm going. I know. I know I'm going out of my mind."

At the next waiting area, we were directed to an examination room. There, a team of psychiatrists, a man and a woman, went quickly from obvious questions about Max to little tests of his perception. They held up fingers for him to count, images to compare. Finally, the woman showed him a red card with a white hexagon printed on it.

"I know what it is," Max said. "It's a card. And I know I'm on a stretcher. And I know I'm in a hospital. And I know this is an hallucination I'm creating." He paused, then rushed on. "I know my friend Enid Sloan gave me this drug. I know none of this is real. I know neither of you is Dr. Rose. I know one of you is male and one is female. I know one of you is white and one is black."

They looked knowingly at each other—they were both white. I studied them more carefully, wondering if Max was still in the tunnel with black orderlies, or if the man's broad Slavic features looked Negroid because of the bluish fluorescent light, or—I was coming around to Max's view, seeing through his eyes—if maybe this man didn't just *look* black but *was* black. Suppose he had "passed," would he now, as that oracle in Emergency had predicted, make sure that Max was put in a cell and left to rot?

"What else do you see?" the woman psychiatrist asked, still holding the card close to Max's eyes.

"I see red."

"That's all."

"I know this is an hallucination."

"What is?"

"The white. The white isn't real."

"I don't believe him," she said to her colleague. "He's deliberately refusing to see the hexagon."

"He's a painter," I said. "The color probably registers more strongly."

"He's not a painter now, is he? Not after what you gave him. You've caused enough trouble. Better wait outside."

"Maybe I should go home, I need sleep. When can I return in the morning?"

"You'll have to sign for his belongings. We'll let you know when we're ready."

In the waiting room I felt as if I'd been banished to a foreign country. Almost everyone was speaking Spanish.

"How long does this take?" I asked the receptionist.

"The doctors know there are other patients waiting." She made a gesture encompassing the people in the waiting room. "They'll be putting him in Observation soon enough."

"And they'll let him out tomorrow?"

"That depends—"

In a moment Max was wheeled past me, heading toward the elevator.

"I'll see you tomorrow," I said, catching up with him. "Sorry about the way this turned out."

He opened his eyes and smiled. "I don't blame you. I shouldn't be here. I should be in my studio. I should be painting. It's not easy—traveling, not working."

About a quarter of an hour later, an attendant returned carrying a hanger dressed with Max's clothes and shoes—that pathetic squeaky pair of shoes—tied by the laces over the hook. He counted Max's money and wrote the amount on a form that already listed the items of clothing.

"What do I ask for when I visit tomorrow?"

"Oh yeah," he replied, handing me a mimeographed sheet containing the ward number and the visiting hours.

I ran down the corridor, down the steps, and out into the night. The city was emptier than a few hours before, more perfectly ready to receive me.

I was up long before I could visit Max, and I was walking south long before the time it would take to get to the hospital. It looked even drabber, more dismal, more forbidding than it had the night before. All I cared about was getting Max out. I could hardly believe that, having wanted to give him a gift of sunshine and oranges—initially, anyway—I had given him this island of darkness.

The waiting room in the psychiatric ward was crowded almost entirely with women—dozens of mothers, wives, sisters, and sweethearts waiting for the doors to open. I tried to figure out why women were so much stronger than men, why critics were so much stronger than artists. It took me a while to realize that, in some other ward there must be a crowd of men—fathers, husbands, brothers, lovers—waiting to see the women waiting behind closed doors.

Now, once again, there was a babble of Spanish. Almost lost in this animated roar, I thought I heard Max calling my name. After a moment, I saw him, in gray hospital pajamas, waving at me. I pressed through the crowd and hugged him.

"Are they going to let you out?"

"Don't know. Dr. Rose hasn't arrived yet. Should be here any minute."

"Any minute! Is he still punishing you for being a naughty boy, taking that bad medicine?"

"Maybe something like that. Everyone's been punishing me . You've no idea. They beat me."

"Who?"

"The attendants. I thought it was another hallucination, but some of the patients said they saw me being punched. I have black-and-blue marks." He started to open his pajama top.

"Maybe you struggled when they undressed you. Maybe, with your sensory perception heightened, ordinary handling—"

"No! I was beaten. My fantasy was something else."

"Max—" I hesitated but had to say it, wanted him to know from me and not from Dr. Rose— "Max *you* wanted to come here, *you* wanted to be punished, *you* wanted *me* to be punished."

"You don't have to tell me. It's what I tried to say last night. It's why I accept what happened, why I don't blame you. It's—" He stopped suddenly and looked across the room. "He's here." Max smiled. "He'll need to tell me too."

A small bald man squinted in our direction, then walked earnestly toward us.

"I don't want to meet him, " I said, hugging Max quickly again. "I don't like him."

"He's *really*—"

"I know. And I'm—Oh, just say I *really* didn't want to meet him." I paused. "You've been hard on me. I'd be harder on him, *much*—him and his *higher criticism*."

I spat out the last phrase, then hurried once again from the hospital. But now I knew—knew even more clearly that the previous night—that traveling with Max was too exhausting. Now I wanted only to help him find a studio and then get back to my own work. There wasn't any doubt in my mind that Max would paint again, that his best work lay ahead of him. At the same time, ahead of me, I could see my words, hundreds and thousands of them, piling up higher and higher—they were already that real, that close, that naked, without even a coat of paint.

Did You Know Gorky? Pollock? Kline?

The elegant young man was wearing a muted mustardy Italian turtleneck shirt of cotton so sheer it looked like silk. The dark hairs on his chest showed through like sculptures, each hair an assertion. Over the shirt he wore a blazer. It was made of green baize which, after many phone calls, his secretary had gotten from a billiard table manufacturer's supplier.

Usually, when his tailor furnished the material (except for cashmere), a jacket cost $250; for this one he asked $225. Through several fittings there had been talk around that. The tailor said baize was hard to handle and wasn't worth anything anyway. The customer, this elegant young man, said that was just the point, that in every business one pays less to have cheap materials worked than expensive ones. This was, after all, a coarse commercial wool. The elegant man thought he had the tailor by the balls. He spent three or four thousand dollars a year on his clothes—not just this year, when things were very good, but every year. The tailor, for his part (pins in mouth, tape measure over shoulder) had a certain bargaining position too. He knew his customer, knew he wanted quarter-inch overlapping seams (not a sixteenth, or an eighth, or what others wanted). He knew how high to take the hookvents, knew just where to notch the lapels, knew the sort of foulard this customer's fantasy demanded—not only as a lining for the body of the jacket, but the sleeves. He knew, in short, on which side the man carried *his* balls (the left), knew the measurement (32") from there to the straight cuffless horizontal line, without a break, above handmade shoes.

They played through the fittings. The tailor reduced the jacket to $215 while adding $10 to the price of antique carved-amber buttons the man selected. Both parties were happy.

The elegant man was still happy as he sat now at home in the green jacket. It always made him happy, more happy than what he wore at the office. And the turtleneck shirt made him happy. And so did his brown wide-whale corduroy pants and maroon loafers. He often thought that the secret of happiness was comfort and he hoped that someday executives would wear what they wanted to the office, that someday clothes like these would be trusted. That was one of the things he envied about artists, that they were comfortable while they worked. Perhaps not as comfortable as he was now, perhaps not wearing materials as unusual, but still during the day there was no tightness around their necks. If they were talented, they put the tightness into their work. He was reminded of that as he looked around his apartment at pop control, op control, kinetic control, a dozen kinds of control that made the whole place as beautiful as good tailoring.

In one hand he held a martini which might, theoretically, have added to his happiness. However, in the other he held the evening paper. The two broke about even, leaving him with the original happiness, the beauty he found in his after-hours environment.

Two rooms away—past the dining room, in the kitchen—he could hear his wife preparing dinner. It, too, would be something beautiful. He could taste it already—game, perhaps, or in-season fish—and the right wine, uncorked, breathing, waiting for him: another example of control. In some ways, he thought, the days were the price one paid for these evenings. Not that the days were so austere—as usual he had lunch at a French restaurant—but, with a customer, there was a limit to how much one could drink. It was another tie around the neck, this one permitting barely a trickle, two martinis, no wine—the head had to remain clear and in control. Did artists drink while they worked? He was still wondering about this when the phone rang.

When there were calls it was understood between him and his wife that he could go on reading and drinking and enjoying his paintings, his clothes, his total environment. She answered the phone. That was part of her job, and besides she liked getting calls—there were never enough for her; he got too many during the day. But, despite this convention, he always stopped everything (the reading, the drinking, the enjoyment). So now he concentrated on the kitchen, two rooms away, wishing his wife would lift her voice, wishing he could have life both ways, audible *and* quiet, the way it was at the office. This time he heard only a blur of sound, indistinguishable words coming from his wife more rapidly than usual, a sort of nervous buzz. Finally he heard the receiver go down.

"What was that?" he called.

She came to the living room wearing her Mod outfit: a striped shirt, wide belt, bell-bottom slacks in a bold plaid. She looked beautiful, like a painting, like an object. She smiled her smile—those lips, those teeth — and said, "It was him again."

"Him" was a painter who had taken a floor-through in the unconverted brownstone next to theirs. He had called twice before, saying that he would like to meet them, had heard a lot about them. They knew right away what he had heard: that they bought art. They checked on him. He was one of those Abstract Expressionists, left over from the fifties, an old Ab-Ex, beard and all, forty or so, out of things. That's what their friends in the know had said.

"I hope you told him we're busy." He knew she hadn't, the way he knew at the office when a salesman botched a contract or a secretary forgot to make an extra copy.

"I couldn't—this was the third time he called."

"Well, what *did* you do?"

"I told him to come for lunch on Saturday."

"Saturday!—that's my day at the galleries."

"So we do them with him."

"Yeah," The elegant man's face lit up. "We'll show him what's really happening."

Although they had invited the painter for twelve-thirty, they began drinking at noon. By the time he arrived they were on their second martinis and playful, ready for amusement. They looked forward to lunch (the fresh salmon in aspic was beautiful, the dry white wine was already chilled) and to their walk up and down Madison (in and out of galleries) and to ridding themselves of the painter they had not yet met and, after that, to getting into bed for their late Saturday afternoon "nap" (when the elegant man was always at his best, more rested and relaxed than during the week).

"I wish he weren't coming."

"Yeah."

The doorbell rang.

"Be nice."

"Yeah."

They didn't have to tell the painter how far out of things—their things—he was. He knew as soon as the door opened. There was that *click-click* in response to his ring, and he was in a stairwell just light enough to let him see the Castelli posters, the cartoon blow-ups, the trembling hard-edge images, everything he hated most in this 1967 world which was moving too fast from inner to outer space. He heard a shrill voice call, "Come right in," and he waited for the rest of it: "the water's fine," which never came. Already, halfway up the stairs, he felt old-fashioned. Perhaps that feeling had been triggered by the *click-click*—he was old-fashioned enough to think that someone should have come down to greet him. With each step he regretted having called these people. Friends had told him that he should, that they were big collectors, and yet he felt already that he wasn't for them and they weren't for him.

The barrel of a gun on a poster pointed at him as he ascended the last step to the parlor-floor landing.

"What would you like to drink?" It was the host's voice, a deeper variation of Come right in, or Come on in, or Come in, or whatever it had been—if it mattered, and it did. But he was already forgetting the stairwell, faced now by original paintings, some hippy-dippy world that was flat on some walls, shaped on others—either way antagonistic to him, as impersonal as that *click-click*.

"A coke, please."

The elegant man and his elegant wife exchanged a glance. It was not entirely one of disapproval, though that is the way the painter saw it. What they were saying, based on three years of marital E.S.P., did have something to do with the painter's not wanting a drink, a real drink, but it had to do also with the way he looked. First of all, his beard was neater, more carefully trimmed than they had expected. Second, his clothes were so conservative, right out of the fifties—not the art fifties; rather, the Madison Avenue, Park Avenue, Lexington Avenue, even Third Avenue fifties of some forgotten world which was buttoned-down, pressed, un-groovy; a world the elegant man lived in weekdays but wanted to forget on weekends. In a word, they found the painter *stuffy*.

Today the elegant man was wearing one of his cashmere jackets, tailored just like the green baize (but falling from his shoulders as softly as a whisper); his wife was wearing a suede suit (which fell more like green baize). They felt *with it* in their Saturday outfits, and they drank one more martini while the painter had his coke.

"What kind of work do you do?"

"Nothing like this." The painter made a gesture as though sweeping these paintings—and constructions, objects on tables, everything here—from his sight. "I hope you'll come and see my work. It's abstract but mostly out of *nature.* " He saw their puzzled looks—it had been a long time since they'd heard that word. "Not that I work directly from nature—I don't set up an easel in the park or anything like that—but there's a strong sense of sky and space in my work."

The elegant couple understood. They imagined a great froth of Ab-Ex canvasses, the suggestion of a skyline in each, sandwiched between lots of juicy paint.

"Did you know Gorky?"

"He died before I came to New York."

"Pollock?"

"A little."

"Kline?"

"Better."

"Are they the kind of painters you admire?"

"I don't admire their being dead." He didn't know what this couple was doing—putting him on, or down, or what. "They were *serious* artists."

That was one of those words like *nature* which the elegant couple had not heard—or even read—for a long time. They smiled their E.S.P. smile and suggested lunch.

During the meal they made jokes about Vietnam, integration, art, everything. The painter sat there, talking very little, passing the wine back and forth between them, smiling when he could. In that he was helped by the work of art on the wall opposite him: a big handsomely framed box of Corn Flakes. He spent some time wondering what they had paid for it and the rest planning his escape after lunch. He had been taught not to eat and run, so he explained that he had a lot of work to do, that he could only go to one gallery with them, and that then he would have to leave.

That left the elegant couple very little time. They wanted to buy something, to show this painter what it was really like to swing, now, in 1967, on a Saturday afternoon.

At the gallery there was a plastic cube full of mirrors glittering under a spotlight. They took it off the pedestal, turned it this way and that, watching the light dance. They asked if they could take it outside to see how it looked in the sun. The gallery owner said sure. The piece sparkled. They asked how much it cost. It was only $250. They said they'd take it, to wrap it up.

They felt they had put on a good show—no haggling, everything done clean and with their sense of style—but when they looked for the painter, to get his reaction, he was gone.

P___: A Case History

P___ is middle-aged, of medium height, neckless, bullet-headed, with features that are unrefined, almost blank. He was stout but has been losing weight for no apparent reason. His skin fits loosely now.

He is in bed beside his wife—inches away, which might as well be miles. They have made love, and now she is asleep, breathing regularly, not as heavily as before, perhaps more contentedly. They are alone together, in their bed, in their room, in their apartment—a series of boxes within boxes, limitations within limitations.

P___ can't sleep. He plays with himself, his penis still moist from his wife. He strokes it gently. Nothing happens. It is tired, this thing with a will, a life, of its own—part of him and yet as separate as his wife, less than a foot away. He grips it more firmly, strokes it harder, teases the tip. Still nothing happens. He tries to shake it awake and alive. He doesn't want to admit that he (it) is getting old or, at least, with each passing minute, older, nearer to death.

He thinks of women at his office, secretaries, filing clerks, receptionists; women he has known; women on the street; women on the covers of magazines; women on the television and motion picture screen. They blur, become faceless, lose their identities in the single identity of their sex. P____'s mind becomes one large collective cunt. He wishes he could possess it, fill it, this collective all with its core of emptiness. But for what? The same humiliating fiasco he would go through if now he awakened his wife, if he weren't so considerate. The irony is dark and dismal.

P____ wishes that the act of love didn't pass so quickly, that he could sustain an erection for longer, for ever, that he could fuck every woman who goes through his mind, through his life, past and future. All this amounts to a single prayer: that God grant him a cock permanently rigid, always at the ready, a tool as tough as leather, as hard as horn, broad and solid as a man's thighbone—or that of a bull. He prays for a great crowing cock.

Images fly through his mind: winged Pompeian phalluses; Leda's long-necked swan; well-hung acrobatic Minoans; long pricks drawn on the walls of prehistoric caves, on scrolls of Egyptian papyrus and of Japanese silk; pricks painted on ancient terra cotta and baked for permanence; pricks illuminated by medieval monks; pricks carved in stone or wood; pricks cast in bronze or precious metals; scrimshaw pricks made from whale teeth; pricks erected as monuments to the living and the dead; pricks worshipped, carried as amulets, used as dildos; pricks reproduced, illustrated, described throughout the history of art and literature; incunabulous pricks; photographic pricks; black-and-white motion-picture pricks; blue-movie pricks; full-color pricks; off-color pricks; pricks wired for sound by Masters and Johnson; vibrating battery-driven pricks, sold in so-called drug- and so-called novelty-stores; pricks that can zoom to the moon....

Despite the loose-formation flying through P____'s mind like so many birds, planes and rockets, all lofty, erect and goal-oriented; despite advances in technology and variations in symbolism; despite everything, the prick itself remains the same, unchanged after thousands of years, whimsical as his own, sometimes hard, sometimes soft and tender as now. That is the reality; the other—the examples from art and architecture, engineering and technology, advertising and mass media—is the dream. And yet ... And yet ... As P____ tells himself these things, he still fondles his prick, wishing it would fill his hand, both hands, both arms, and then soar altogether out of reach.

He removes his hand, wanting to sleep and forget this limp thing between his legs—and in his mind: there, a collective image as hollow as the cunt.

P____ turns over. His prick is soft beneath his stomach. He is ready, finally, to settle for far less than a monumental prick of stone or for one that stretches ten feet across a scroll. He would settle for his youth, when he was able to masturbate five or six times a day; he would settle for the youth of classic Greece, a boy, with a perfectly ordinary hard-on, running perpetually around a vase. And yet ... And yet, again, he does want it to be forever, to be eternal. He prays.

The clock rings. P____ emerges from a world of snakes, swans, goats, bulls. His hand slithers from under the blanket, flies to the night table, butts the alarm switch, kills the sound. He is awake, quickly as always, precisely one hour from his desk at the office. Carefully, so as not to disturb his wife who has barely stirred at the sound of the alarm, he gets out of bed and shuts the window. A magnificent erection bulges out of his pajamas, and he regrets that it too will pass, die, like last night's, like those of all the other nights and days. Once again he wishes that it could be forever, that it could be as efficient and dependable as the rest of him which he presents at the office.

He tiptoes to the bathroom and quietly closes the door. In the mirror he hardly sees the tired, loose-skinned, lumpy image of himself. His eyes focus on his cock, erect as before, young, alive, and rosy. He tries to urinate but the erection won't let him. He presses his stomach, tickles his buttocks, turns on the water in the sink, concentrates as if in a doctor's office, fears that he may be late to work. As he becomes anxious, his prick relaxes slightly, asserting its own life. He tenses his stomach muscles, pressing, pressing. Painfully the urine forces its way out. The stream is thinner and longer-lasting that usual. It burns. In the toilet bowl, it seems to boil.

P_____ steps over to the sink and prepares to brush his teeth. He is surprised that his prick is as rigid as before pissing. He studies it more closely than his face. It intrudes as if to grab the toothpaste on the edge of the sink, as if to reach even farther up and take the brush from his hand. As he shaves, his prick is there, poised in the mirror, watching him, wanting to get in on the act, some act, perhaps wanting now to grab the razor. P_____ shaves mechanically, hardly looking at his face, aware mostly of his prick, still at attention in the mirror.

He starts to put on his underwear, first a T-shirt, then elasticized briefs which don't have the strength to hold his cock down. They bulge like a sail in the wind, a very steady wind. He becomes anxious again, knows he can't go to the office like this. He remembers his wife, slips out of his underwear, joins her in bed, kisses her lightly on her closed eyelids, her ears, her neck, her breast; strokes her back, holds her close to him, makes her feel that great thing between his legs, between hers now.

She responds, opening her legs and mouth, saying, "You want me, you really want me, don't you?"

"Yes, yes," he replies, forcing his way into her. "I need you."

"What time is it?" she says, asking the sort of question that might another time have made him go limp.

He turns toward the clock and tells her.

"You'll be late."

He replies by driving the shaft of his prick as far into her as it will go. She writhes. Her pelvis churns. Her breath, slightly foul from sleep, comes in short hard gasps. Her juices begin to flow, reluctantly at first and then in rapid spurts. There is no stopping her. Her movement is relentless. She groans like a motor at maximum performance.

P_____ is pleased by her pleasure. She seems to be asking for more, more, more, as her hips hop beneath him. He rides her, wanting to give every drop, ounce, pint perhaps, in his balls, stating the message of their heavy content as they slap against her buttocks. We have so much to give, they say. But nothing is given. Ejaculation is as difficult now as pissing had been just a short while ago.

He pumps on, wanting not only the orgasm straining to be released within him, within her, but wanting also to get to work on time. His wife, churning beneath him, ceases to exist. He thinks about the orgasm which won't come, the breakfast he will miss, his tardy arrival at the office, his appearance there. He says new silent prayers, makes new pacts with ancient gods: If only this orgasm is granted, if only he can be released from the rigid prison in which he finds himself, he will never again ask for anything. The previous night, and so many nights before, his wife had satisfied him. Now he can satisfy her but not himself.

He withdraws. She opens her eyes, smiles, says just one word, "Wow!", turns over and goes back to sleep.

His erection is harder, bigger, stiffer than ever. He can barely get his briefs on. They tug at his crotch. He takes them off again and gets an athletic supporter. This works better. It is stronger, more elasticized. He lifts his cock so that is rests close to his stomach, almost parallel to it rather than perpendicular. But still there is a great rock-like bulge straining at the jock. This is the best he can do, more comfortable, he's sure, than strapping or taping it to his leg the way studs do in pornographic novels, that world in which everything and everyone is controllable, that fantasy world.

He is late. As he finishes dressing, he wonders if he should call the office and tell them—what?—that something has come up. He smiles. That is just the sort of vague explanation his secretary gives. In his case it's precise, too precise. Never complain, never explain, he has been taught. But not complaining is difficult: he won't explain.

He hurries to work. With every step he is aware of the aggressive pressure in his jock. He is led, pointed to the office, by this leashed thing just an inch or so from his stomach, always that little bit ahead of him, impossible to overtake. Young girls, old girls, mature women come toward him, pass by quickly on the way to their jobs, noticing neither the bulge in his pants nor the need in his eyes, noticing nothing. This is both a relief and a disappointment, like having a pimple on his nose—huge to him, almost invisible to the world. But the analogy won't stand up (another joke, another smile); the scale of his present affliction is so much greater. He feels the hugeness of his cock, painfully pressing forward.

In the elevator he is thankful he is late. What would it have been like, at nine, pressed against all those bodies? How would he have explained his condition as some switchboard operator screamed "Rape!" or some male filing clerk yelled "Queer!"? As it is, with only four others in the car, he removes his hat and holds it over his crotch, still believing that everyone knows. At his floor he races past the receptionist and a corridor of secretaries, including his own. His greetings are perfunctory. He wants the protection of his desk.

There he gets through the morning, keeping the walnut top between himself and the world. But always beneath the correspondence, contracts, budgets, operating statements; beneath the words he dictates to his secretary and those he speaks at conferences and into the phone; beneath everything is his prick nagging at the jock and the jock nagging at him. That is the real problem, beneath, but also above, all the others. That needs attention, more than next year's prices, more than fluctuations in the value of the dollar.

Fortunately he doesn't have an appointment for lunch. When the executives who are free ask him to join them, he says he has work to catch up on. He buzzes his secretary and orders a sandwich and coffee to be sent in.

"Anything else? A slice of pie?" She waits, pencil poised over stenographic pad.

Hair pie, a nice juicy wedge of hair pie, P____ thinks, imagining them going down on each other, as he says, "No thanks."

He watches her leave the office, studies the movement of her hips, wonders if —

What would The Secretary's Manual say? *Be cooperative at all times. At the executive level, you will be asked to perform personal chores such as addressing Christmas cards, minor shopping, the payment of bills, the sewing on of buttons, etc. These tasks should be done willingly. They contribute to the executive's efficiency, they free him for other work...*

What does that "etc." mean? How far does it go? How far would she go? She has done all the other things in the manual, all the other wife jobs, why not this? A little blowing to follow the sewing, a job done easily, under the desk, during lunch hour. He could promise her a raise —

When she brings in his lunch, the executive area is empty. Again she asks, "Anything else?"

Well, yes—the words run silently through his mind—I'd like to discuss your salary with you. Please shut the door. I'm going to be requiring—

Still in his mind, he feels her out, himself in—with his tongue this time. And he imagines hers, moist and tender on his cock, licking it, soothing its painful throb.

The actual dialogue is as brief as before. He says only, "No thanks." Again he watches her leave his office. Again he studies the movement of her hips. Until now he has never understood the psychology of rape. He begins to understand. And as he eats his lunch, he thinks of her eating hers and wishes she were eating him instead.

The coffee seems to drop right to his bladder. He goes to the executive john, chooses a stall rather than an open urinal, tries as hard as he had at home. The agony is more intense now. It burns like a licking flame, inside, out of reach. Even touching his penis is painful. He cannot aim it at the toilet bowl. It points straight ahead.

He must bend his body to avoid splattering the wall. But that becomes academic. There is no splatter, no splash, not even a thin stream, not a single drop. There is only the pressing pain of urine trying to escape, the throbbing blood in his cock blocking that escape.

P____ puts his cock back in its elastic halter, wondering if he is entirely responsible for his predicament, his pain. If he willed it up, why can't he will it down? If his past prayers were answered, why not the present ones? He imagines a computerized heaven in which prayers are answered in the order of their receipt. Perhaps the computer, like his prick, is jammed, jammed by all those other men wishing for perpetual hard-ons. The lucky ones, P____ thinks, they don't know what they're missing.

From his office he calls his internist, who is as close to God as P____ can get. He tells the nurse that this is an emergency. She says she will fit him in. P____ smiles. The world is filled with cruel jokes.

The nurse escorts him into the examination room.

"Undress and leave a urine specimen in the container in the washroom."

"That's the trouble. I can't."

"Oh! Well, the doctor will be with you in a few minutes. He'll fix you up."

Another joke, P____ thinks as he undresses. It's a relief to take the jock off. His prick springs forward into a horizontal position, rigid as ever. He wonders what the nurse would think if she walked in now. Something like that had happened years before, when he was being shaved in preparation for an appendectomy. That nurse had given his erection a sharp tap with two fingers—a mini-karate chop—and it had subsided. He wishes that his present situation was as simple.

While he waits for the doctor, P____ tries to urinate. He turns on the sink faucet. He flushes the toilet. He concentrates on the sound of the rushing water. Leaning over the toilet, with the container in one hand, he presses his bladder with the other. He tenses his stomach muscles. He tickles himself. Once again nothing helps. The container remains empty.

In this clinical atmosphere he examines himself—his prick, his painful prick—more carefully than before. Although the shaft is absolutely stiff, the tip is rather flaccid and insensitive, unresponsive to tickling or pressure. The pain seems to be at the base. He is still examining himself when the doctor enters.

P____ forces a grin, somehow expecting a broader one in reply. Despite his pain, there is a comic side to the situation: he feels rather ridiculous, standing there with his hard-on, like a character in a dirty joke.

The doctor doesn't smile. The nurse has told him that P____ can't urinate. He focuses immediately on P____ 's penis.

"How long have you had this?"

"All my life," P____ replies, trying again to break the ice, to cut through the doctor's brusque clinical manner.

"This trouble, this erection."

The doctor's tone is urgent, he has no time for jokes. P____ assumes that he is rushed because of squeezing in this unscheduled appointment.

"Since early this morning."

"How long since you urinated?"

"Then. With difficulty. Pain."

"What about sexual intercourse?"

"This morning too."

"Was it pleasurable?"

P_____ tries to remember. It seems long ago. "No. Mechanical. I thought it was a way of—you know—getting rid of it. What else does one do with an erection?" Again P_____ offers a smile. Again it is ignored. "I didn't come."

"Have you felt any sexual desire since?"

"Fantasies. My secretary blowing me. Even thought of rape, though seduction's more my style."

And once again P_____ smiles without response from the doctor. Instead there's yet another question:

"But don't you remember if there was real desire? Try to recall."

P_____ tries, puzzled by this line of questioning which is more like a psychiatric examination than a physical one. His prick hurts. It's what needs attention, not his mind. Finally he says:

"I don't think so. I guess I just wanted to use her. Like my wife. But for God's sake, I haven't been able to take a leak since morning."

"I can take care of that. I'll catheterize you, but I'm afraid there are other things I'll have to do first."

"What?"

"Oh, some blood tests."

The doctor's casualness sounds forced. His "Oh" hangs in the air, like the smell of lysol.

"Do you know what I've got?"

"I know it's some kind of priapism. I don't know the cause. If I knew, you wouldn't need the tests."

P_____ is relieved. He has a vague idea that priapism is mental, a sort of male nymphomania. Now he understands the reason for all the doctor's questions and the need to correct his own wishes and prayers. Yes, he will stop equating the life of his penis with his own life and with life itself. He will —

But the doctor continues: "What you have is very rare. I've never seen a case before. It may be common as a fantasy but not as a medical fact. There is usually a thrombosis—a clot blocking the passage of blood from the penis." He takes out a prescription pad and makes a quick sketch, including directional arrows, of an artery feeding what he calls "venous sinuses in the corpora cavernosa" and of veins removing the blood from them, finishes by drawing an X over the veins. "The clot," he says. "That's what we've got to find the cause of."

P_____ winces as the needle enters his arm. He watches the syringe fill with blood, identifying this blood with that in his penis and praying that it, clot and all, is being sucked out. He cannot yet realize that he is sick, physically sick, beyond blood-letting, beyond prayers, beyond magic, perhaps beyond hope.

The pain caused by the hypodermic is minor, no more that of a bee sting, compared with the catheterization. P_____ can barely hold back his tears as the thin lubricated rubber tube is inserted and probes inward toward the bladder. He feels violated, tortured in a way that would make him admit anything—things done or not done. After further probing, a stream of urine splashes noisily into the specimen jar. The removal of the tube is less painful than its insertion, but, though smooth and lubricated, it still feels like sandpaper—perhaps a finer grade now—being drawn across naked nerves.

The doctor continues the examination. "You've lost considerable weight."

"Yes, I've been working hard and playing a lot of squash."

"Trying to prove that you're getting younger?" the doctor asks rhetorically and rather gruffly. "I wish—" It is obvious that he is about to deliver a lecture, but he changes his mind and scribbles a prescription. "This is a mild sedative, to relieve your discomfort. I can't prescribe anything else until I get the results of the tests. I'll call then. Meanwhile, probably best that you rest in bed. Take as few liquids as possible."

P_____ returns to an empty apartment. He can't rest. He can't concentrate on reading or television. He lies in bed on his back with his knees up protecting his penis from the slight pressure of the sheet and blanket. He looks at the clock, wishing it would move ahead faster; at the phone, wishing it would ring; at the clock again, still reading 3:22. He has had an erection for just over seven hours—maybe more—seven waking hours. This is as close to forever as he wants to get.

He listens for the sound of his wife's key in the door, wishes she would return, wants to talk to her but doesn't know what he wants to say, wants to talk to anyone but doesn't want to tie up the phone, realizes that the doctor can't possibly have received the results yet, thinks of calling his secretary but doesn't know what to tell her either. There's nothing to say, nothing to do but wait. It's 3:24.

P_____ tries to reconstruct the medical examination, to piece together the doctor's words, spoken and unspoken, his facial expressions and the lack of them. He is convinced that the doctor knows or suspects more than he lets on, masks the knowledge and suspicions with his professional manner, just as P_____ himself does when negotiating. P_____ knows now what he wants to say to his wife. He wants her to promise she will insist that the doctor tell him the truth or, if he will only tell her, that she in turn will tell him, that there be no censorship, no professional games.

And P_____ wants to tell his wife something else too, something that he has always found very hard to say. He wants to tell her that he loves her, that he has always loved her even when he was with other women. He wants to explain what it was like in hotel rooms in distant cities when the working day was over and he thought of her and the children (now grown) and knew no way to express his love except with his prick.

Another parade of women marches through his mind, not like last night's, not office acquaintances or movie and television stars, but only women with whom he has slept. Nevertheless, as much as the others, they are strangers and, more than the others, they are fuzzy and indistinct in P_____'s memory. Now as he tries to separate them, each becomes a different burden of guilt. He can feel their weight in bed.

The list is long, the weight crushing, but he cannot blame these women for his present painful punishment. Once again he blames himself. He lifts the top sheet and studies his prick, erect between his thighs, arrogant, willful, defiant, daring him to knock it down. He imagines the doctor's cool voice: "I'm afraid there's only one cure—amputation. You yourself said the only thing to do with an erection is get rid of it." "But not that way," P_____ screams in his mind. There is no smile now. He is as unresponsive to his humor as was the doctor an hour or so earlier. He has told a dirty joke to himself, or on himself, which fell flat.

Lightly he touches his penis, runs his fingers up and down its length, presses a little harder. As at the doctor's office, there is pain at the base and some softness at the tip. The rest, except for veins, is smooth and firm. P____ feels no pleasure in his touch, no desire for a more masturbatory caress. He drops the sheet.

It is almost five, the hour at which ordinarily he would be going to play squash. He wonders if he will ever play again. How could he play in his present condition? How could he even go to the club? Undress? Shower? What could be more embarrassing? Only to have no prick at all, as in that fearful joke, that amputation fantasy. He lifts the sheet again, closes his thighs over his penis, sees only pubic moss or underbrush, misses that great tree which grew in the midst of it, hates its absence, parts his thighs, hates it presence, hates himself, hates his pain.

If his condition persists, there are other things he will no longer be able to do, summertime things, the things he likes best: walking on the beach, swimming in the ocean and riding waves to shore, playing tennis, sailing..... As each of these past activities moves through his mind, he edits out the other participants, except for his wife. He and she are alone on the beach. They find an isolated stretch for swimming. They give up doubles (except perhaps with their children, to whom he will have to explain his condition). They sail alone (except, again, maybe with the children). P____ feels close to his wife, closer than during intercourse last night, much closer than this morning. Again he wants to tell her how much he loves her. Where is she?

She doesn't arrive until close to six, 5:43 to be exact. By then P_____ has gone through a long imaginary session with his tailor. How casually the man asks, "Which side do you dress on?" as if he had never asked before, as if P_____ had not been coming there for years. "The left," P_____ replies, "but maybe you should leave some room up front." "I noticed." "It's some rare disease." "One we all want." "You don't. It's called priapism. You're not Greek. I'm not either. Not as far as I know. Maybe this small part." P_____ laughs mechanically. "You've lost weight." "Another symptom." "Not so bad either." P_____ feels they are raving, that he himself is not making sense, not communicating, that the tailor is still envious. For a moment P_____ wishes the disease were contagious. Then he wonders how, if he can't communicate with this tailor who means nothing to him, he will ever be able to say what has to be said to his wife or children. He can't imagine talking about pain to anyone but a doctor.

Throughout the rest of the fantasy fitting, P_____'s wife is there, where she has never been before, dimly reflected in the three-way mirror, murmuring the announcement of her presence—a preference for blue, for slightly wider lapels. Beneath her whispered comments, she is saying without words, that she knows he needs her, that that is why she is here in this forbidden territory, that she has heard him call, that she is waiting.... And yet it takes so long for her to really appear—until 5:43, *really*.

"What's the matter?" she asks when she sees him in bed.

"Oh"— that casual, medical *Oh* again—"I seem to have something called priapism." P_____ lifts the bedding and shows her.

"I'll fix that."

"No, not this time. I'm waiting to hear from the doctor. He took some blood tests."

"He thinks it's serious?"

"Afraid so. That's something I want to talk to you about. Before he calls. I want to know. I want him to tell me the truth. And if he won't, I want you to. He was cagey at his office."

"Maybe he doesn't know."

"He knows what I've got. He said he didn't know the cause. Beyond there being a clot."

"No point in imagining things. Are you allowed to have a drink?"

"I guess one would be all right. Trouble is I can't take a leak without being catheterized."

"Then we'll wait. We'll celebrate when the tests come in negative."

"You have a drink. Have one for both of us."

"I'll wait."

"Don't be a martyr."

She looks hurt. P_____ thinks that now may be the time to say he loves and appreciates her. "Sorry —" he begins, but even that one word is difficult to get out, and just then the phone rings. They both reach for it, but P_____ is closer.

"Fine, dear ... You? ... Yes, she's here but we're waiting for an important call. Can she call later? ... Fine." He hangs up. "Fine. Everything's fine."

"There's nothing to be angry about. She didn't know you were waiting for a call."

"Sorry," P_____ says again, with effort. As if programmed to the word, another bell rings, the front door this time. "God, you're not expecting anyone, are you?"

"No. I'll get rid of whoever it is," she says, leaving the bedroom.

P_____ recognizes the doctor's voice as he greets her. That's enough. P_____ doesn't have to listen for the note of solemnity. The fact that the doctor came instead of calling says everything.

They are whispering now, but P_____ doesn't need to hear the words either. He knows that they mean the same thing as the doctor's visit. P_____ 's impulse is to call them into the bedroom, but that can wait—the official professional word or words. He hopes only that his wife is doing what he asked, getting the truth. The whispering continues. It is not like other whispering he has heard in his life. Now they have to be talking about him, his prick. And they can't be saying anything good. Finally they enter.

"How's the patient?"

"You tell me."

The doctor hesitates. "I never know what to say at times like this. I've been talking to your wife. She says you want the truth. That's what most patients say. But I don't always believe them. A few really want the truth. Some want part of the the truth. Most want only hope. Only hope. Of course that's a lot. But there are new drugs, better ones coming out all the time —"

"My wife told you what I want. I can tell you what I don't want. I don't want bullshit."

The doctor looks startled. "All right, the truth then. But it's not pretty. And it's not funny," he adds pointedly.

"I want it anyway. Straight."

"The tests show you have leukemia."

There's no misunderstanding this, no confusing it with a mental disease.

"I've reserved a room for you at the hospital. I want to have more tests taken. I want specialists to look at you. We'll do everything we can."

"How long?"

"It's difficult to say, almost impossible. Months, half a year, a year, maybe longer. It depends on so many things: how acute the leukemia is (the additional tests should show that), how you respond to medication, what new medication comes along—many things."

"Did you know all this when I saw you?"

"No. I was pretty sure, but —"

"What?"

"What good would it have done to know sooner?"

P_____ is tested, examined by specialists, jabbed, probed, x-rayed. Fluids are removed from his body, others are injected into it. His responses to medication are continually measured by temperature, pulse rate, blood count. Something is always being put into his mouth, his arms, his urethra. A nurse or doctor is always touching him, "just trying to help," as they say when he becomes irritable.

Much of this irritability he saves for his wife, who sits hour after hour waiting for some word of hope. Though P_____ appreciates her devotion, he hates her pity, the solicitousness which oozes from her like tears. He wishes she would go away and not be there to witness his humiliation. But he can't put this into words. His eyes, dull and angry, say it. His silence says it. If, trying to make conversation, she asks petty questions, he looks at her as if she is stupid. If she asks the real questions, those that are on both their minds, he mutters, "Ask the doctor," usually no more than that. The facts, in answer to the real questions are: He feels neither better nor worse—well, perhaps a bit weaker from remaining in bed and eating little of the tasteless institutional food. Otherwise, there's nothing new. No change. His penis remains hard and painful. For three successive days he has had to be catheterized. "Am I supposed to say I feel great?"

His wife begins to spend more time in the waiting room. However, she is with P_____ when, on the fourth day, the internist tells him, "We've been afraid to use a conventional anticoagulant because of the risk of hemorrhage, but now that the case is fully diagnosed, we can give medication that should relieve the priapism."

P_____'s eyes become brighter. He can hardly wait for the medicine.

"What is the full diagnosis?"

"Acute leukemia —"

"But you said you can relieve it."

"The priapism. And that may recur. We have no cure for leukemia. You said you want the truth."

The doctor leads P——'s wife out of the room. P_____ hears them talking as they start down the corridor. He imagines a still more complete diagnosis, a still more acute leukemia, a still more final word: death, the word, the fact his doctor must be telling her to prepare herself for. The phrase "acute leukemia" runs through his mind like blood. The addition of the adjective is a terrifying subtraction of time. And yet later the doctor tells him he can return home. That in itself sounds hopeful.

"What am I allowed to do?" P_____ asks.

"Almost anything you want. Just don't tire yourself unnecessarily. What do you want to do?"

"I was thinking of going to the office for a few hours a day."

"All right. But don't push yourself, don't feel you have to go. If you're tired, call in and say you're not coming."

From the following Monday until Wednesday ten days later, P___ is at his office from ten till noon. He tells everyone he's had some kind of blood infection but that it's clearing up. He is surprised that the short walk there is so tiring. He arrives as tired as he used to leave. He loses track of his dictation. Again and again he tells his secretary, "Please read that back." But as she does, his mind wanders. It is difficult to believe that not so long ago she interested him. Her hips are just lumps now, nothing that could give him pleasure. The words of contracts drift, float away. These, too, he must hear again as he repeats the words aloud to himself, trying like a child to seize them. The sound of the air-conditioning distracts him, works on his nerves, like a catheter. The chill penetrates, hums in. He is always cold.

On Wednesday an erection materializes on the way to the office. He thinks of returning home, but goes on, protected by a raincoat which he always carries now, even on the sunniest, warmest days. He reads and rereads a small pile of mail, recognizing that less and less is being directed to him. He dictates haltingly, remembers that the doctor has said not to push himself, and finally tells his secretary that he's not feeling well, that he may have one of those bugs that are going around.

The doctor seems to accept P___'s diagnosis: "Yes, probably that. These viruses attack when one is most vulnerable."

The medication is doubled. The erection departs. Without catheterization, it softens easily and painlessly.

For the first time in weeks, P_____ makes a small joke. While fondling his penis, he calls it "my measuring rod."

His wife winces, forces a laugh.

That is his last day at the office. He loses weight more rapidly and must go to the hospital for a transfusion. After returning home, he says for the last time that he would like to spend a few hours at business, but by the next day he feels too weak to go, the desire is dead, all desire is dead.

The bright wallpaper in the bedroom seems as drab as the walls in the hospital. His wife might as well be just another nurse. When he looks at her, he sees that she, too, is thinner, that she appears strained and forgotten. He forgets her.

She brings him his lunch and notices that he hasn't opened the newspaper.

"What have you been doing?" she asks.

"Just waiting."

"I had to fix it."

"I don't mean for lunch."

He eats one bite and pushes the tray away. The food tastes bad, but in fact it is not the food he tastes but something persistent, like lead in his mouth, some base metal. She takes the tray and eats a little of what's left before throwing the rest away.

There are more transfusions, almost commutational visits to the hospital. P_____ lives off the blood of others. His existence is a passive cycle of blood drained and replaced, of clots and priapisms formed and dissolved, of drugs taken and evacuated. He is half his former weight. He can no longer bear to look at himself in the mirror or at his penis, too frequently rigid, swollen with bad blood. Now his only prayers are for death.

Several times he thinks of speaking to his wife, of saying what he has to say, words dimly remembered. At last, feebly, he calls her to his bedside, takes her hand without the strength to really grip it.

"Sorry," he begins. But can't go on. There is no strength left, no other word left. He dies with the erection he had wanted for so long, for ever, never having told his wife all he had to say.

Candide's Garden

Two twenty-one? Is it possible? I break a twig from a nearby bush; scratch the four digits of the present year, 1980, into the earth; then 1759, the year of my birth; and subtract. Yes, 221. But, scratching deeper now, I still add a question mark: the facts of my birth are so mysterious.

Although it is clear that my father was Voltaire, I do not seem to have had a mother. Emilie, Marquise du Châtelet, Father's great love, died ten years before my birth, after having a daughter by the Marquis de Saint-Lambert. And Father's niece, Mme. Dennis, almost twenty years younger than he? Well, the erotic letters remain: "I kiss your pretty bottom ... " and the rest—but no indication of inspiration like that offered by the brilliantly creative Mme. du Châtelet. No, my birth must have been as immaculate as Athena's from the head of Zeus—"a miracle" I would call it, without wanting to offend Father.

There are other mysteries—for example, the date of conception, which most scholars believe was November 1, 1755, when Lisbon was destroyed by earthquake. They trace this event from the poem Father wrote on the subject, through numerous references in his correspondence, to the publication of the book about me in which it again appears—an incubative period of about four years. However, at publication I was presumably in my teens, living in the castle of Baron Thunder-ten-tronckh and old enough to be interested in his daughter Cunegonde. Therefore, I consider the Lisbon earthquake simply a convenience, another drop in Father's bucket of evidence against the optimism of pre-established harmony. I would rather push back the date of my conception than attempt to push forward, against overwhelming bibliographical evidence, the date of my birth.

At least one more dating problem remains: my age at the end of the book, after Father has, in effect, given me his life. Was I 65, as he was, when I was born? Or was I—more likely, based on the time my adventures would have taken—in my late thirties, as he was when he met his great inspiration Mme. du Châtelet? Father often spoke proudly of her translation of Virgil at 16; of her studies in mathematics, physics, and astronomy, in order to translate Newton's *Principia*; of her interest in music —spoke in a very different, much more adoring tone than that which he used in speaking of the actresses he had known in his youth or that plump niece with whom he later settled in Geneva at his villa Les Délices. Perhaps, however indirectly, my own aptitude for arithmetic does come from Mme. du Châtelet. Or, of course, it could as well have come from Father himself.

And finally there's the difficulty of physically determining my age. Like Father in his youth, I was very thin, seemingly frail but actually strong and energetic. And like him, by middle-age—given his life, his suffering—I looked old, cadaverous and mummified, the way I look now at 221, when my ailments are real. After all,

I saw combat, survived the Lisbon earthquake, lived these things up close about which he wrote mostly at a distance. However, unlike him, I never used my physical appearance to defend privacy or work—never pled impotence to avoid a woman, or illness to avoid a visitor, or deafness to avoid a tedious discussion, or near-blindness to avoid reading another's manuscript. He manipulated his health—when convenient was almost crippled, or almost deaf, or almost blind, or almost dead, and then, minutes later, was out in the garden, spotting weeds from far away and uprooting them with the agility of a child.

The parade of visitors from all over the world was itself an affliction. At Ferney—where, during the two decades between my official birth and his official death, I knew him best—not everyone was James Boswell. There was, for instance, another, less meritorious visitor from the British Isles whose reception still makes me chuckle:

Father said to a servant, "Tell him I'm sick."

The man wouldn't leave.

"Tell him I'm dying."

Still the man insisted.

"Tell him I'm dead."

The servant returned to say that the visitor wished to pay his last respects.

"Then tell him that the devil has carried me off."

The devil. Evil. Not an heretical Manichean invention but a fact of life and death.

Yes, Father defended himself very well. If he hadn't, he could not have accomplished what he did. Not only the plays and tales and pamphlets and articles and histories and philosophical books which I saw him

write during the two decades—well, 19 years, really—
when I knew him. But the physical work I saw him do—
the gardening, the farming, the planting of woods; the
building of roads, canals, bridges, factories for the manufacture of silk and pottery and watches, workers' homes.
And, perhaps most important, the defense, not of himself, but others—Calas, the Sirven family, La Barre—
those who were persecuted and then tortured on the rack
and the wheel.

I think of the next century: even Zola's defense of
Dreyfus was a comparative skirmish in the war against
prejudice and superstition. Nevertheless, Father had to
defend himself and had to invent a son like me, with a a
name as open as mine. If he hadn't, someone else would
have, as he said about God. I am the part of Father he
could not expose to the world, except as fiction.

Candide. Later, Captain Candide. What a fantasy! What an invention! And yet Father, too, was
virtually motherless (his mother died when he was 7).
He, too, had a seemingly harsh father. He, too, gave
himself a name, finding in Arouet l(e) j(eune) the ana-
gram—if u is taken as v and j as i—that would become
Voltaire, possibly an abbreviation of his nickname "Le
Volontaire," Master Willful, as I am Master Open—each
an exaggeration of a single aspect of our characters.

I think now of Molière who took a *nom de plume* a
century earlier. But how much more Father and I have
had to pay for our names—he by being cast forever in a
role that is too complex, me in one too simple.

When Father was re-baptised François-Marie de
Voltaire, at the age of 22 but already the rising literary
genius of his day, there is little doubt that he was express-
ing both youthful aristocratic pretension and worldly

ambition, like Honoré de Balzac in the next century. However, Father, some nine years later, at the height of his success, suffered an insult for this that he always told me changed his life.

I can see him, hear him—eyes wide apart, bright as coals burned deep into that monumental brain; nose sharp and pointed as a dagger; lips pressed thin, then opening over toothless gums—as he spoke in a voice both precise and pained:

"It happened in the last days of 1725. I was at the opera with the actress Adrienne Lecouvreur when Le Chevalier de Rohan-Chabot came up to me and drawled, 'M. de Voltaire, M. Arouet, what *is* your name?'

"It was a stupid insult from a stupid man, a soldier who never fought a battle and lived with no distinction but his great name. Perhaps the old Huguenot duke, Henri de Rohan, turned in his grave. I chose not to respond. But the next night, the same situation, the same actress, the same insult.

"This time I said, 'I do not drag a great name behind me but do honor to the one I bear.'

"The Chevalier raised his cane. I put my hand on my sword hilt. Mlle. Lecouvreur obliged us both by pretending to faint."

Father chuckles, then becomes grim:

"A few days later I was dining at the Duke de Sully's—a relative of Rohan's, you know—when a messenger asked for me at the street door. Rohan's coach was there, and I should have been warned, but before I could do anything six of his men grabbed me and began beating me with rods. The Chevalier sat in his carriage laughing. Even people in the street laughed. What was a middle-class poet to them, compared with a Rohan? It was the same when Lord Rochester had Dryden beaten. Perhaps worse because Rochester himself was a poet— of sorts."

A faint smile, then the grimness again:

"I escaped, returned battered, begged the Duke to come with me to the police. But now, despite an intimacy of ten years, he laughed too. Perhaps the Queen herself laughed, though she had just recently given me a pension. Anyway, I could get nowhere with the Ministry. There was nothing to do but challenge the Chevalier to a duel. Although I had a sword, I didn't really know how to use it—well, maybe against a cane wielded by an idiot, but not against another sword. I took dueling lessons, found a second, delivered the challenge." Father sighs. "The next day I was arrested and placed in the Bastille— my second visit, much briefer than the first. Candide, do you know what I thought about while I was there, before requesting exile in England?"

I must have looked blank.

"Power. Every minute. Every day. Power. And of course, with it, freedom. I thought I had earned these with my pen. I thought I had The Crown's ear. But that is gold. Now I wanted what Rohan had—yes, gold itself, and servants, and homes, and the freedom to move. And later I got these things. It's easy for someone on the outside to say I write for money, but no good writer does. Not just for that. There are easier ways to make money. My investments, my speculations, even my manipulations—these were just for money, just for power, just— but remember what I did with my money at the end, how much of it was used to start those industries at Ferney, how much to defend Calas and the others, how much to house refugees. Remember, and then you, scrawny as I

am, duel with anyone who attacks the name of Voltaire—
or that of his son Candide."

I felt pride in his pride, still do. We are the
survivors in the family —he at 286 me at 221. But now
I carry his fame as once he carried mine. Who cares any
longer about his *Oedipe* or the *Henriade*, his *Brutus*, *Mérope*,
or *Mahomet*? They are dead. Even *Zadig*, Father's love-
liest child, most charming brother and rival of mine, so
much wiser and purer than I, even he who moved more
quickly through the world (in even fewer pages and
shorter chapters), even he, my favorite sibling, is forgotten, he who was both sage and knight in white armor,
brilliant solver of riddles and brave master of the lance.

Sometimes I wonder why he hasn't lasted as long
as me and become as popular, but the explanation is not
hard to find. It is in the distinction, the uniqueness of his
body and mind. He is a god, and the world only pretends
to love its gods, then discards them. In me the world
loves itself. Zadig's adventures were as interesting as
mine, but they moved in a different direction. Because of
his educated talents, he married a queen, became king,
and at the end lived the loftiest of Father's youthful
dreams, enjoying peace, glory, and abundance, govern-
ing with justice and love. In the course of his story he asks
many questions, as wise men do, but only once expresses
my sort of human muddle. That was when the angel
Jesrad, talking of this world and its injustice and suffering, tells him to "cease contending with that which is to
be worshipped," meaning, of course, the world itself.
And even then Zadig spoke just one word, potent thought
it was. Speaking through Father's lips, as I do, he said
only, "But—."

I moved in the direction of Father's later life—not toward the heights but toward the earth, and growing and building things on it; not toward a queen but toward my worn-out, often raped, and now ugly childhood sweetheart Cunegonde; not toward a kingdom but toward a small farm, peaceful but not glorious, where abundance is relative and hard-earned. There I too had my say—like Zadig's, distilled from a lifetime's search for hope. On his way to a throne, he said, "But—." Kicking a rock, one of many which would have to be cleared, I said, "One must cultivate his garden."

How much weight those five words carry, the weight of my life and that of my friends, all created by Father. Kickings, beatings, battles, destruction, rape, torture, sickness, mutilation, murder, disembowelment, shipwreck, drowning, earthquake, hanging, flogging, slavery, plague, bestiality, cannibalism, robbery, lying, cheating, prostitution—all these shaped those concluding five words of mine, my destiny, the cure for what went before.

Yet within two years after the publication of my book (and his), a second part appeared, a sequel to *Candide*, which falsifies my life (and his, again). Sometimes this Part Two is attributed to Father by careless scholars and translators, sometimes even placed between the covers of our book. However, it is actually the work of an obscure contemporary hack. There is enough internal evidence to refute its authenticity. Yes, adventure is piled on adventure, invention on invention, but without Father's style, grace, or wit. Speeches are too long, physical descriptions inaccurately detailed, transitions awkward. Too often chapters end "as we shall see in the next chapter" or, worse, "he spoke what follows."

But the physical descriptions most clearly identify this fraud. As all can see, I have never lost a leg. Nor has Pangloss lost an arm (an eye, an ear, and the tip of his syphilitic nose suffice). And can anyone believe that Father, realist that he was, would have had Cunegonde recover her beauty? Finally, Part Two's ending—my idle happiness in a Danish title and in wealth—betrays all the values Father established in his own life when he settled at Ferney, and in mine when he placed me in my garden. Furthermore, remember Father's admiration for Volume One of *Gulliver's Travels*. He called Swift "the Rabelais of England, but a Rabelais without the rubbish." However, when he read Volume Two, he said, "the second parts of romances are so insipid."

Fraud breeds fraud. Yet another hack has written a still fuller sequel to my life: *Candide in Denmark*. And doctoral dissertations have been written on my progeny, as well as on Father's. It's all too much. If any reader has an edition of *Candide* which contains a sequel, please rip it out and, if you like, put this autobiographical fragment in its place. Or read Flaubert, an enlightened student of stupidity who loved Father as I do. He ridiculed those who thought of Voltaire as the antichrist; those who could not hear his name without referring to his "diabolical" grin, his *rictus*; the same people who spread lies about his end, saying that by then he was eating his own excrement. Just retribution, they believed. But as we know—you and I and Flaubert—if Father was eating anything, it was his own heart.

So much for Father's end. My true end is here in my garden, that analogue of work—the work one is capable of doing for oneself and for others, two different kinds which sometimes overlap.

The sun is setting on the Bosphorus. Striated bands of pink and blue shimmer beneath Istanbul's minarets and domes, gigantic in the distance, even to my weak eyes. I sit here at day's end, tired but content, knowing that Cunegonde is in the kitchen making pastry while her old servant sits on her single buttock doing laundry in a bucket between her veined legs, and Paquette, who gave Pangloss his pox and is now too old to earn a living on the street, embroiders with great delicacy, despite arthritic fingers. Pangloss himself continues to argue with Martin about whether this is the best or worst of all possible worlds, both philosophers too stubborn to adopt the position at which, with Father's help, I have arrived—simply, that this is the world, neither Pangloss' heaven nor Martin's hell in which "man was born to live in the convulsions of distress or the lethargy of boredom." At least now, while arguing, they assist Friar Giroflée with his carpentry, making small pretty things at night, like bowls and stools, saving the heavier work for day—the buildings, wagons, and other improvements to the farm. Cacambo, once my servant and now my friend, helps them with construction, or me with my gardening. Even now, under moonlight, he is completing a trench around the largest stone remaining in the garden. Tomorrow or the next day we will move it, all eight of us.

With the main house and surrounding walls, stables, coops, pens, workshops, and sheds all completed, we have been working on a project, perhaps as useless, perhaps as much a luxury, as writing this scrap of my life. We are building a place for meditation, a chapel as simple as the one Father tore down at Ferney, before replacing it with that classical building, half church, half theater, which bears the inscription *Deo erexit Voltaire* (Voltaire built it for God). Ours says, as accurately, *Voltaire erexit Candide.* These words, like his, are carved in stone; Cacambo worked for weeks on them. Inside, carved in wood, are two other inscriptions: *There is something of divinity in a flea* and, opposite this, the much more famous *Crush the infamous thing,* by which Father meant, as I do, *superstition.*

The entire chapel is built of natural materials. Although Father made fun of the Senator, Lord Pococurante, I feel as the Senator did: I do not like art—and I include architecture—which is an imitation of nature but only that which is nature itself. Friar Giroflée has carved benches out of solid teak. I have placed a copy of Houdon's marble bust of Father in the almost finished building. Often I sit before it, like a chip from that skinny block of stone, almost lost in shadow.

I wave a momentary good-bye to Cacambo and go there to think in the dim light, remembering with difficulty words of Father's spoken to others, repeated now aloud by me:

"*Building and planting are the only activities that can comfort old age....*

"*Had I cleared but one field and made but twenty trees flourish, that would still be an imperishable boon....*

"*What really matters is that this poor species of ours should be as little miserable as possible....*

"*The further I advance along the path of life, the more do I find work a necessity. In the long run it becomes the greatest of pleasures, and it replaces all one's lost illusions.*"

And now, as often, I remember too, with difficulty too, words which he had characters speak directly to me. For example, I repeat those of the wise Turk who said, *"Work keeps at bay three great evils: boredom, vice, and need."*

Again, Father's voice becomes my voice, a single voice echoing in the chapel. Yes, during the past two centuries I have lost many of my illusions. I have seen revolutions Father did not live to see and wars beyond even his imagination, rape beyond human scale—the rape of earth and sea and sky. And yet, as I sit before his bust and his few carved words, obscured now by near-darkness, I suppose he becomes impatient when true, so true, to my youth, I tell him what I have learned.

"Father," I say, "I am happy to be almost deaf: I am spared so much babble.

"Father, I am happy to be going blind: I need not see what man does to his fellow man.

"Father, I am happy to be partly crippled and short of wind: I am not forced to leave this pleasant spot and go out into the world. You remember, you had the King of Eldorado tell me long ago that when we are comfortable anywhere we should stay there.

"Father, I am happy to be impotent: Cunegonde has ceased her demands.

"Father, I am happy to be bald: the sun warms my head and the moon cools it.

"Father, I am happy that my memory weakens: there is so much I want to forget."

A tear, shimmering in the moonlight, rolls down Father's smooth marble cheek. It must have rained earlier. I'll ask Friar Giroflée to check the roof.

But my own words are no more than a digest of felt thoughts. They sound small as I sit, surrounded by timber and stone erected to Father's memory, that monument of words. Once again, I think of the eighty or so volumes of his collected work, seventy-nine of them forgotten, and say:

"Father, you too must forget them. Perhaps I alone am your monument—I have learned from you. But monument or not, like you, I am mortal, frail, as transient as your daily games of chess and mine, less frequent, of pitching horseshoes. And like you, I am unafraid of death. (How many times you said that to me, to your devoted Dr. Tronchin, even to Boswell, a comparative stranger.) So, I will complete this chapel, knowing that it may topple in an earthquake and that the words inscribed on it may vanish. Father, I wish we could share a cup of coffee—it's so good here in Turkey—your favorite drink, the one that made your mind race and the world seem tolerable."

Now it is really dark. I call Cacambo and tell him it's time for sleep. Tomorrow, as usual, we must prune and weed and then find a spot for this heavy stone. I see it already placed, opposite that elegant bust, balancing it in natural harmony.

Duplex

I don't know what to call my room. Perhaps that's enough—"my room." It's not exactly a study, though it contains the desk at which our daughter used to do her homework and where now I pay bills, make dates, clip recipes, take care of the thousand things that make my husband's life seem so efficient. Here, on the upper floor of our apartment, I phone or write the words he prefers not to be bothered with, words that smooth the surface of our life in the social space below—thank-yous, acceptances, regrets, congratulations, condolences. No wonder the drawers bulge, spilling their contents across the desk top and onto adjoining sills, shelves, the floor itself. Letters, photographs, catalogues, magazines, treasured birth announcements and obituaries —bits of life and death—accumulate in boxes and bags until they too spill into irregular piles, a volcanic paperscape; the stuff— some of it raw, some of it packaged—for an autobiographical collage. (Is there any other kind?)

I've emphasized paper. There are also more durable materials here —things bought at antique shops and auctions, commemorating other people's lives and not yet part of my own; things I'm still looking at, trying to find a place for. There's the tortoiseshell frame, framing nothing till I can find the right picture as well as the right spot (perhaps in the powder room?). The frame, edged and monogrammed in silver, with initials that might at a glance be mine, is temporarily on the spool table I want to put in the front hall, if ever I convince my husband that, having lasted a century or so and survived the trip from a New England mill town to New York, it's not now likely to collapse. No, the large industrial spools that form its legs are as perfectly joined as vertebrae. How poised they look supporting that picture frame which might have been mine in another life, is mine in this one.

Also on the table, flanking the frame, on one side there's a pair of candlesticks made from artfully twisted Civil War bayonets and, on the other, a humidor of layered cigar-box wood. I keep the lid up so I can see the pattern of cigar bands lining the inside. That was a difficult decision. Closed, the humidor is pretty too. Each layer of wood, one slightly smaller than the one beneath, is notched along the edges which rise like a ziggurat to a small oblong platform where there's the touching dedication, in separately carved letters, TO DAD/PORTSMOUTH PRISON/1916—the year of our birth, my husband's and mine.

It's all touching—the scraps people saved that I now save for them. And I haven't mentioned the copper-strapped Roycroft chest, set off like an island on that hooked rug. The chest is crammed with quilts—another vision, another use, another geometry of scraps. The early-20th-century cereal-box dolls sitting on top, their plump stuffed legs reaching toward me, are a recent purchase, bought as a collection and therefore not yet as individually familiar as my other things. So far, MISS

FLAKED RICE is my favorite. I lose myself in her large sad eyes, those dark pools of lithographic ink printed on cotton older now than my own skin.

I could go on, piece by piece, around the walls, across the floor, into the closet, describing my affairs with things, my hidden loves. And yet, my most hidden love—that enigma, my husband—is my subject. I wish he didn't call my room "the depot" or "the warehouse"— three maidless maids' rooms serve that function. Even "study" would be better. He can see I work at my desk. There's no need for him to scoff at its Victorian scrollwork.

"The whole room is scrollwork," he said early one evening, after returning from his club. "Nothing stays in place. Nothing moves in a straight line. Everything twists and turns. It makes me nervous."

He twisted. He turned. He left.

Nervous is nothing. How does he think I feel in his office (once a cozy library; then our son's room, when he lived at home)? I followed my husband; passed the lovely arrangement of prints, samplers, antique valentines in the hall; descended the stair surrounded by shop signs, old political posters, early American flags; plunged after him into his environment—desk top clean, reference books shelved in tight ranks, magazines stacked chronologically on coffee table of shiny steel and glass, walls bare except for a map of the world and an economic chart I've never learned to read—everything, the world itself, chilled by blue fluorescent light. My temperature dropped. I shivered, remembering this room when our son occupied it, filling the walls with pennants, nudes, rock stars, actors, athletes.

"It was human then," I protested, "as human as my room, as human as the rest of the apartment."

"The rest of the apartment?" He smiled coolly. "You've wrecked it. I've given in too many times. We had an understanding once—checks and balances, mutual approval—but now the place is yours, all the clutter, all the mess. I wanted serious art, serious furniture. You decorate as if you were running an orphanage. Here, every foundling has a home."

That hurt, partly because it wasn't true. Not even as a metaphor. I wanted another child. He said no. Later I wanted to adopt one. He said no again.

"Your idea of serious is an operating room."

He studied me studying his office. His eyes became more blue, frozen in this awful light. Even his lips looked blue beneath his blue-gray mustache. When finally he spoke, he spouted ice.

"We'd better separate."

I waited for more, then asked the obligatory question, "Is there someone else?"

"No one."

"Something else? Something you want to do?"

"Nothing."

"But you don't love me?"

"I didn't say that. I said we'd better separate."

"When?"

"As soon as the work can be done."

Again I waited. He glanced at his phone, making clear he wanted to begin "the work." Maybe with a call to our lawyer? Maybe with one to the movers?

I left his office, went to the living room, automatically switched on the lights, curled on the tapestried Gothic Revival couch, felt comfortable there on real furniture, looking at other real furniture (bentwood, horn, Mission, wicker) and at real art on the walls (the Navaho blanket, the portraits of Abraham Lincoln and Booker T. Washington framed in the windows of a dainty log cabin—no maps or charts here), real books on the shelves (those meant to be read for edifying pleasure), real light (from the sun and from polychromatic Tiffany and Pairpoint lamps). Sinking deeper into the couch, I tried to puzzle out my husband's "executive decision," as he might have called it. There's probably a better term in one of his reference books—maybe in some guide to mental illness.

His words weren't a surprise. They might have been, even a year ago, when he retired—mandatorily, at age 65—but not now. There'd been hints. Odd, how at first I thought we would become closer. With the children grown, gone, involved with their own lives so far away, visiting us only about once a year—almost always, it seemed, to present a new grandchild—I thought we'd fill that empty space, that distance, with each other. And when he retired, I hoped I'd become whatever business had been to him, at least a way to pass the day, a way to get through lunch. I imagined him sleeping late as I do, then having a light breakfast with me in the kitchen before going to our son's room, his new office, to read the paper and his mail. With that and my chores done, we'd select a small restaurant off the beaten business track, walk to it, window-shopping all the way, and during drinks and lunch decide which shops to visit in the afternoon.

It didn't turn out that way. He continued to rise early, long before me. He continued to go to his office, the present one as if a thousand employees were waiting there for his command. By the time I got up, the paper was refolded beside my coffee cup and grapefruit, his office door was shut.

I don't know what he does in there till noon. Sometimes he emerges with a handful of letters to mail—nothing more than that, and fewer as the months pass. Always, after reviewing our plans for the evening, he goes to his club for lunch. Except for two weeks, beginning with our anniversary—the fortieth, the first since his retirement—our communications were brief till evening. But then, the morning of that anniversary, he spoke silently and eloquently. My half-grapefruit, always cut and scooped by him after he made the coffee, was decorated with two sections of orange embracing half an upright banana. On the newspaper there was a small box containing an Art Nouveau brooch of a woman's head with golden hair resembling mine as it once was and, inside, the question, scribbled on a card, "Can we last 40 more?"

I pinned the brooch on my bathrobe, admired it in the emergency make-up mirror hidden behind one of the kitchen-cabinet doors, felt happy till I compared that small smooth untarnished face with my own. This mirror was busy once when the kids and their friends used the kitchen door. Now, when the bell rings unexpectedly, it's mostly dealers delivering one thing or another; they look at me as if I were an antique. I read the card again, wondering if the emphasis was on "we" or on "40 more." In the mirror it was on "40 more," and my answer was "no." I began eating around the banana, saving it for dessert.

That day at noon, when my husband appeared, I kissed him, thanked him for the brooch, went on giggling and appreciative, about the grapefruit's decoration. Perhaps I went on too long. For those next two weeks every morning there was something different on my grapefruit—mounds of cherries, berries, or grapes in the center; slivers of peach, pear, or apple arranged like the petals of exotic, but always geometric, flowers; slices of banana; wedges of pineapple; combinations of all these. Each day I looked forward to what my husband would find in the refrigerator and transform.

"It's like anticipating the morning headlines," I told him.

"Don't you dread them?"

"No, they're the high point of my day," I replied, meaning the decorations, not the headlines.

I never thought he'd misunderstand, think perhaps I was being sarcastic, but the decorations stopped.

Conversations wind in my mind as the smoke from my cigarette drifts, looking solid against the light from the sun sinking over the Hudson. But with this difference: The smoke diffuses and disappears; the conversations linger. They're twisted too, reshaped by time, maybe misunderstood, but still they stay, in my head, and in this very living room, the room in which—it seems years ago—we used to talk about so many things, important then, I thought, to both of us, now only to me.

When I cooked more often—for him, the children, and our friends—he once said, "It's an unnecessary complication."

"Cooking?" I asked, sure I'd missed the point.

"Yes, most food's better raw."

I must have looked surprised but waited for evidence I knew he would present.

"I don't suppose there's any argument about fruit or vegetables."

I didn't argue, though my mind wandered through fields of potatoes, broccoli, asparagus, artichoke.

"Compare fresh clams with clams Casino, oysters with oysters Rockefeller," he continued.

"Convenient examples," I argued then. "What about lobsters? Crabs? Fish? Meat?"

"I said most food. By cooking I meant with sauce. Broiling, boiling, steaming don't count."

My fields of vegetables were ruined—scorched, then drenched in steaming rain. "Salt? Sugar? Lemon? Vinegar?"

"They don't count either. Sauce! Sauce is what I'm talking about. The hours you spend on making sauce."

Those were the hours he spoke of then. Other times it was of the hours I spent selecting wine.

"They're wasted on me. I like beer with seafood, beer with steak, beer with chicken, beer with chops." I knew his list could go on, but he stopped, switched to a related topic. "And I prefer a glass. I like to see what I'm drinking."

He didn't have to explain. He'd done that—first with a collection of German steins I'd bought; later, with the English pewter mugs; still later, with the grainy aluminum ones from the Depression, their handles cast as streamlined, near-sexless females nudes. When we're alone I give him a plain glass. Like the brandy snifters and gold-rimmed cordial glasses, the steins and mugs are saved for company. But still he persisted:

"One kind of glass is enough. And one kind of plate. And one kind of silver—or steel. Preferably steel.

Everything shouldn't be divided into breakfast, lunch, and dinnerware; stuff for us and stuff for company; stuff for the kitchen and stuff for the dining room. You wear yourself out deciding what to use when, where, with whom."

It was a favorite argument of his, which made no sense. Sometimes, especially when we were going out and I was late, choosing among possible outfits, he'd say, "You have too many choices, too much of everything. There's no need for different clothes for morning, noon, and night. I don't have sport shirts, sport jackets, sport suits. I choose clothes that work for everything. One kind of suit. One kind of shirt. If it's hot, I take off my jacket and roll up my sleeves."

"You can't roll up the sleeves of a glass."

I think I won that round. For years he'd been quoting, "Less is more." But I know less is less, have told him so. I also know a few other things, unspoken but obvious to any woman, perhaps too obvious for the mind of a man. I know: Infinity is finite. I know: Eternity stops. I know: I have, therefore I am. I can see those words—a collector's creed—on my tombstone in the past tense: I HAD, THEREFORE I WAS. Of course my husband doesn't believe in burial, thinks it's primitive and inefficient. I'll have to sneak into my grave.

I smile, wince, light another cigarette. Its glow relieves the darkness of my humor. Again I watch the drifting disappearing smoke, seeing a difference between it and the lasting things hanging on the walls. The Navaho blanket is a century old. Though I've hung it away from direct light, it continues to fade. But, even if slightly softer, the colors are still bright; and the diamond pattern, shifting back and forth as if on the loom, dazzles the eye. The portraits of Lincoln and Booker T. Washington on the same wall, away from the harsh light of the setting sun, have yellowed with the years since Reconstruction. They're on cheap commercial paper, torn from a magazine or newspaper, and yet reminders not only of these men themselves but of someone—an ex-slave probably—who saved and cared. How many hours he or she—or perhaps a couple working together—must have spent building this small cabin from which those faces peer.

More than once my husband said, "It's time to wash the walls," words as offensive as "the depot" and "the warehouse." What he meant was, time to sell the things he didn't like (for example, the log cabin) and others on which big profits could be made (the Navaho blanket, the Tiffany lamps).

The first time he used this expression, I thought of things to say about his lack of taste. It was really that, not bad taste but a blankness there. As to his greed, perhaps a habit learned in business, it was harder to attack—I'd lived off it for many years. So I said only, "I love what I buy, always will."

It was a simple oath of loyalty, and yet he took it, to himself, for more. Months passed before he spoke again of washing walls. Then I replied, "Before selling, I'd wash the walls with my own tears."

"You must learn to let go," he said as if talking, long ago, about the children.

"Letting go is death."

Finally I think he knew I didn't want to wash the walls. More months passed, months of words, mostly forgotten, even by me.

As I reached for still another cigarette, he entered the room—six feet of present silence interrupting past conversations. Then he spoke:

"We'll be happier living together separately. At first, blocking the stair seemed the easiest solution."

He paused. I tried to imagine separating the two levels of our apartment with a concrete slab—the stairwell destroyed; the display of shop signs, posters, and flags destroyed too, at best crowded by that oppressive slab.

"I reached the building manager," my husband continued. "He said they've given permission before, always conditioned on an agreement to restore. We're only talking about a few thousand dollars."

"We? You and the manager, you mean. You talk about money. What about the space itself? The posters? The flags? The signs? And, assuming you intend to give me this floor, how do I get to my room? Do I have to take the elevator?"

"I thought of that. I want you to be happy. There's an alternative —"

"Yes. Leaving things as they are."

"Almost." He paused again, dramatically this time. "I was studying the layout upstairs. I went into the maids' rooms. If I had them, knocked out the walls in between, took most of the corridor, that could be my space. With the bath back there modernized, the laundry converted into a small kitchen, I'd have everything I need, a sort of studio apartment. Just one partition near your end of the hall and I'd be self-contained."

His logic was fierce, almost unassailable. And I understood his need for a project. For the moment, I asked only, "How'd you get in?"

"The rooms weren't locked."

"No, I mean in, to move around."

He smiled. "I didn't get far, but I could see enough. Most of that stuff could hang here." He looked first directly at the space between the blanket and the log cabin, then glanced at other empty spots, as if anything could go anywhere, as if hanging took no care. "If not in this room, on other walls—in your floor and a half.... Sell the furniture and what you can't use. Or give it to the kids." I sniffled, blew my nose, dabbed at tears. "Your floor and a half," he repeated. "Maybe ... and three-quarters. I've been generous." He studied my face. I felt more tears sliding down my cheeks. "You'd better wash up and get ready for dinner. It's late. Do you know what you'll wear? It won't be easy to get a cab."

Even before the alterations began we became closer. There was no choice. We had to work together. We cleared the maids' rooms and carried furniture, lamps, antique bronzes, paintings in period frames, countless cartons of forgotten things down to the dining room and placed them there, temporarily, against the walls. We removed the prints and samplers and valentines from the hall and stored them in his present office, where they, like so much else, would eventually hang. I saw that room of his in a new light, already incandescently warm. I could see his map and chart replaced by things with texture, the touch of the human hand. I could see a different table, different chairs, different shelves, all mellowed by time. I could see places for the candlesticks, the tortoiseshell frame, the humidor, the dolls. Everything would be arranged with care, with

love; made misleadingly haphazard, warm again. I
lusted for his room.

A temporary wall of Sheetrock, taped at the edges,
was put up, separating his part of the upper floor from
mine. Behind that—barely muffled later by the permanent wall—the noise began, the sledgehammers opening
up his space. Always I awakened at eight, when the
workmen arrived, and sometimes I saw my husband
briefly as he finished breakfast. He seemed more chipper
now, looking forward, past the paper and the mail, to
daily inspection of the job. It filled out his morning. I
went with him once at the beginning, trudging through
piles of rubble and clouds of dust, thinking he was insane
to choke himself now and crowd himself later, but at the
same time remembering the room that would be mine.
"Is that what you mean by washing the walls?" I asked.
He smiled a trifle condescendingly, as if he thought I
finally understood. Before leaving him to take a bath, I
said, "I'm going to wash my walls." His smile spread.

Later, when the job progressed, beyond cement
and plaster, to paint, it was still a choking tour, but
cleaner, and hopeful with sharp, anticipatory smells. My
husband led me through more quickly now, saying,
"One kind of tile in the bath and kitchen." His eyes swept
over unrelieved surfaces of glazed white. "One kind of
carpet in the rest of the space." Two men were on their
knees at the end of the corridor laying tacking strips. "No
scattering of rugs." Of course he didn't have to tell me
that. He's a one-kind-of-everything man, and I'm his one
kind of wife.

Finally the work was done. Kitchen equipment
and a bed arrived. Porters from the building, not speaking the embarrassing questions I could see in their eyes,

moved his furniture from the old office to the new space. Except for the bed, a functional built-in unit, everything looked as it had—clean, cool, blue-white.

"Would you like my humidor?" I asked. "It would look nice on your table. It's the kind of thing the room needs."

"Needs? Our needs are different. I keep my extra cigars in the refrigerator."

I began fixing up his old, my new room. Things fit fine, as I knew they would. All I *needed*—that word my husband teases me about, but there is no other—all I *needed* was a proper place to put the dolls. I had become accustomed to them sitting on the Roycroft chest. They *needed*—*wanted*, if he prefers—another place like that, something more solid-looking and supportive than a table. I realized then that I don't really like tables, don't like their typically scrawny legs straddling empty space, don't like that waste of space. (The spool table and others of bentwood and horn are exceptions; they're sculpture.)

What I found was a vintage Vuitton steamer trunk, its body scarred and encrusted with labels, its cracked handles still dangling worn tags—a relic that whispered of its own survival through time/space (hinged like the trunk itself). From cartons I removed commemorative plates, ashtrays, match strikers ... unwrapped them, reacquainted myself with them, re-wrapped them, placed them lovingly in the drawers on the left side of the trunk. On hangers, in the space on the right, I hung folded quilts and homespun blankets, hidden too long in cartons. I closed the trunk; propped the dolls on top, MISS FLAKED RICE in the center; decided they looked better with the trunk wide open and their legs hanging over the inside. Now the folded edges of the quilts and blankets were visible and, on the other side, the stately stack of drawers. It was a composition any artist would have been proud of, but still I wanted more—perfection, I suppose. I rearranged the dolls, shifting MISS FLAKED RICE to the left. I opened drawers to create a sense of steps leading to her. I turned tags this way and that, bent them slightly, wanting touches of red and blue.

One tag showed the *Normandie*, her three stacks slightly slanted back, billowing stylized smoke, as her sharp prow cut through crisp blue waves. Another tag, in arresting red Art Deco lettering, bore no image, only the message, printed on both sides, NOT WANTED ON VOYAGE. Perhaps these cruel-sounding words sold the trunk to me. I felt as close to them as to the trunk itself; they applied not only to my things but to me. I wondered about the couple (their names were on the other tag), whose last trip must have been on the *Normandie*. Where, among their ports of call, a jumble of labels leading nowhere, had they been just before this tag was tied? Perhaps on safari, then moving on to some cold climate? Or perhaps skiing and then going someplace warm? Did they continue without the trunk, on some other ship, some other voyage ... lasting, say, some forty years?

The questions were interrupted by the phone. It was my husband calling from his new quarters to confirm our dinner plans before leaving for his club. "I'm in your old office. It's about finished. As much as any room can be." I giggled. "I want you to see it."

"I'll pick you up at seven."

I began thinking about what I'd wear. I wanted to be ready. I wanted to have time to show him the room.

Seven hours later, when the doorbell rang—on the hour, as I knew it would—I was in my black silk suit, waiting with hair combed, make-up on, Art Nouveau pin in place. He smiled. (In response to me, I think. I'm not sure—he's been so happy since moving out.) His mustache lingered on my cheek. He made drinks. We touched glasses. I took his hand and led him to my new room.

For a long moment, he stared so silently he might have been at the Frick or Metropolitan. Finally he said, "It's like your other room. I guess it's what you wanted."

"What you wanted."

He was silent again, perhaps tracing the room's history from library to son's room to office to now. He pulled at his mustache, tugging an idea from his mind. "Maybe we should start over and knock out the wall. You don't really need this room."

"I never said I did." I took his arm, led him to the trunk, lifted the red-lettered tag. "Your message—I mean, the message you gave me."

His eyes became misty as if covered by a sudden fog at sea. "Maybe we should ... knock out the wall," he repeated.

"No, I couldn't go through that mess again. This arrangement's fine."

He looked at me with ancient fatigued desire.

"I need you," he said. "What you've done doesn't always make me nervous. Sometimes it's ... restful."

"Visit. Visit whenever you need to, whenever you want."

"Won't you visit me? We need each other."

"Need?" I asked, challenging the word as sometimes he did. I was no longer sure what it meant. "Need?" I fought back tears, not wanting to spoil my make-up and make us late.

Eskimos

Winter reminds me of my wife, of the world she studied, devoted her life to—the world of the Northwest Coast Indian and the Eskimo: a cold world she devoured, as if so much snow, on field trips, in museums, in her own library and in others like igloos. When she was alive I barely looked at what she read and wrote. I had my own world—the commodities market—moving in faster, more heated cycles than hers. But now it is comforting and revealing to study her books, papers, stacks of photographs, and the few tools, weapons, and carvings scattered around her study.

Often, after the children left home more or less permanently, I'd bring a sandwich to her at noon, half expecting to see her wearing slit wooden goggles to protect her eyes from glare and wind. More than I realized, she was a hunter too, hunting facts and artifacts as Eskimos hunt seal and caribou. Coming out of a trance, her concentration broken, she'd squint at me, at the work on her desk, back again at me—that repeated, uncontrollable squinting, a tic by the end of her life—complaining suddenly that the price of books had gone up so much, the price of everything, the price of life; or, just as suddenly, beginning to argue as if I were one of those outsiders who'd destroyed her tribes, perhaps part of the negligent audience she tried to reach with words.

"You understand, these people, the things they made, the songs they sang, are not just anthropological curiosities. They're clues, criminal evidence. In Alaska it happened long ago, the rape of the land by the Russians, the English, the Spanish, us. Greed and lust ruined the Coast all the way to Alaska." She'd stop, remove her glasses, leaving the imprint that, like the tic, seemed permanent toward the end. "I'm oversimplifying. They're different cultures—the Indians and the Eskimos. The Indians themselves, half a dozen or more." And she'd list them—tribes I've never really gotten straight but, to her, as separate as the countries of Europe.

Yes, at times she lectured. I wish she lectured now. I wish I could actually hear the impatient, argumentative, political rasp of her voice. On the printed page, it's quieter, inflectionless, perhaps too polite, too elegant; perhaps, like her, quite dead. The best words may be those she collected—images really ... of "skin boats" ... of a child smiling "with two teeth like a little walrus" ... of the moon, now new, now full, "following its old footprints in the winter sky" .... Part of a song—this one, unlike most, transcribed originally, I see, by Knud Rasmussen—makes me sad as I try to sing it, breathing hard:

> *My tongue merely joins words*
> *Into a little song.*
> *A little mouth,*
> *Curling downward at the corners,*
> *Like a bent twig*
> *For a kayak rib.*

Their songs, she said, were always accompanied by dancing, clapping, drumming. I sing—try to—for her, for what she knew of what they knew—not just words but *things, things* as simple and as simply joined: different commodities from mine, truly raw materials—driftwood, bone, tusk, tooth, skin, sinew, feathers.

Still breathing hard, I look at a shaman's mask I gave her long ago. She loved it, caressed it, treasured it more than any gift of jewelry, more even than the equally rare whale-bone necklace I'd given her earlier. True, she wore that often, but this she *looked at* almost always while she worked. Placed now, as then, above the bookshelves on a wall of her study, the mask's goggled eyes stare at me from an all too human face, carved in deep relief, with teeth bared and, protruding from the neck, a bird's head holding a walrus in its mouth. Where ears might have been, pierced hands reach out, hands of which she sometimes spoke—or, yes, lectured.

"You understand," she'd say, flattering me once again, "when they hunted, some game was *supposed to* slip through their grasp—to multiply, to assure the food supply."

I remembered other pierced hands, collected in museums we visited together, illustrated in books and catalogues on her shelves. Some hands are pierced by feathers, some by beads; some have only empty holes, like these. I look at my own hands, not nearly so old as those extending from this mid-nineteenth century mask, but old enough. Mine tremble—knuckles raw and red; veins blue; liver spots all earthy brown, joining one another in clusters that look like dirt. Time was the artist who made my hands. Time pierced them too. But the holes don't show. Only I know what slipped through.

Her, first. Could I have stopped that? Got her to leave her desk? Smoke less? Walk more, breathing deeply as I do? Could I have made her a different woman? Made myself an Eskimo husband?

The children also slipped through my hands. Like two cunning Eskimo hunters, described by my wife, they started together, walking as one, in step, bodies touching. Then, approaching their prey—me, their mother, both of us—our daughter, the younger, dropped into a drift of snow and hid, with arrows ready. Our son walked on, armed too ...

I stop, look again at my hands, fight self-pity, fight the images that come to me from my wife in her grave, fight anthropology. It's all a losing fight.

Our son is an Eskimo. His life is boats. More than a sailor, more than a fisherman, he lives off the sea, finds not only his food there and on the beach but also fuel, tools, building materials, utensils. When he was young, I thought he wasn't paying attention. He turned his back on books, museums, "curiosities." But he saw, he heard. He watched his mother, listened to her. I was the one who paid too little attention. In the sixties, I called him a dropout, a loner, tried to interest him in trade and profit, challenged him to compete, told him he was afraid. Now I'm afraid to be alone, and I envy his independence.

Our daughter turned the other way, took the academic fork of her mother's path. She studied; received honors and degrees; thinks, like her mother, that the Eskimo was murdered—packed first in fur, then in the ice of libraries and museums, more recently, in oil. She hardly sees her brother, hardly recognizes him for what he is. Recently, when I remarked, "His life is a field trip," she shook her head, said only, "Oh, Dad," but clearly meant "Poor Dad," as if my brain had gone soft. Well, this library will be hers. But what can I give my son?

There was a third child—a boy, born blue. I wonder what path he would have walked. Perhaps one in between—like his brother, letting some fish get away; like his sister, trying to hold everything in her head. Or a middle path like mine—eventually strewn with a dead mate; distant children; relatives and friends, also dead or distant?

I look at the mask again. It speaks to me in my wife's voice, reminding me that for her, for our children, for the Eskimo, for the bird and the walrus, it is the species, not the individual, which counts and must survive.

My mind leaks. Like my hands, my memory is pierced. Those I love die or travel far away. I lost them as I lose facts, figures, things. And why? To multiply? To assure the eternal supply? To guaranty a natural balance? Is that nature's considerate scheme, the scheme Eskimos —with their clever predatory tricks, their paired hunting, their wolf-killers and seal-scratchers—understood so well? Is that my wife's argument? My children's now, in their different ways?

I wouldn't argue if they were here. I'd put on the mask. I'd sing and dance. I'd clap and drum. Perhaps I will anyway. Sound reaches far. There's magic in this mask. It may bring them back—its friends, its relatives, and my own.

I think, when I give the books to my daughter, I'll give the mask to my son. "A gift must move," the Indians say.

I carry a chair to the bookshelves, climb up on it, reach for the mask, hold its hands in mine.

Mickey

My wife and I, in the corner at the near end of the banquette, are finishing our first round of cocktails when Michael Hoffman enters the restaurant. He is with an elegant blonde, a head taller than he, even in her low-heeled shoes, and at least 30 years younger, perhaps as much as 40. His eyes meet mine as he passes our table, and there's the slightest flicker of recognition—no pause in his jaunty step but a historic glancing nod down and back at me—as he proceeds to the other end of the banquette.

"He seemed to know you," my wife whispers.

"That's not Mickey Hoffman's style. It's more like seeming not to know. Actually, we met when we were kids. But he doesn't always greet me this warmly."

My wife smiles. "Did you have a fight?"

"No, nothing—he just struts through my life, always a couple of steps out front. At summer camp, he was a brave when I was a papoose, then a warrior when I became a brave. At prep school, he was two forms ahead; at college, already an upperclassman when I arrived." I pause. "Yes, I've known Mickey a long time. There are Michaels who are Mike, and there are those who are Mickey. He's a Mickey. Always was. You can understand, with a cute name like that, my thinking I knew him better than I did."

She turns to her left, looking for a waiter while simultaneously studying Hoffman and the blonde. "He is rather cute," she remarks as I motion for another round. "Not to mention her. I never would have guessed he's older than you."

"Part of the problem—that he's older and looks younger."

"That wouldn't account for the iciness—a meager two years."

"At the beginning—at camp, say—chronology was important. And at school, he must have had a patina of sophistication I resented. Of course, he was also good at the things I couldn't do, things that are easier for a small man. High diving. Show jumping. And, later, he was a whiz on the dance floor."

"He looks like a dancer. Did he ever dance professionally?"

"Mickey! Only on Wall Street. I've heard he made a lot of money. Ahead of me there, too." I sip my second martini. "And way ahead in marriage."

"What makes you think they're married? She's not wearing a ring."

"I don't know anything about them. But he's been married four or five times. I know that. Probably between marriages now. Or preparing to be."

"It's silly, your knowing so much about him and his not recognizing you. It's—" she searches for the right word—"unequal. I have an idea," she continues, while finishing her drink. "Why not send him a note? You know, identifying yourself."

Dear Michael Hoffman (if you are Michael Hoffman), where do I know you from?

☐ Camp Straight Arrow
☐ Buxton Academy
☐ Dartmouth College
☐ The New York Scene

That seemed to do it but, before signing my name, I add a couple of fictitious flourishes:

☐ The Princeton Institute for Advanced Study
☐ Rockefeller University

When the waiter serves our next drinks, I give him the note to deliver to Hoffman. Watching Mickey over the tops of our menus as he and his friend read, my wife and I wait for him to smile, to begin checking the squares, the first four at least, then perhaps the last two—for laughs. Yes, after half a century, giggling recognition will finally be established. We'll all laugh over the bottle of wine he'll send to our table.

They read the note quickly. His bland expression changes. A shadow of irritation grays his pink cheeks. His brow furrows. His jaw sets. He ages before our eyes as he crushes the note, puts it in his pocket, says a few words to the blonde, and gets up from the table.

The easy, youthful grace of his arrival in the restaurant is gone. He approaches us aggressively, arms flapping as if he doesn't know what he's going to do with his hands, hit me or strangle me.

"What's the matter?" he says in a voice loud enough for the blonde to hear. "Has your memory gone?" He crowds the table. "You know damn well I was at Straight Arrow long after you. And Buxton. And Dartmouth."

"That's not the way I remember it," I reply quietly.

"Remember! You don't remember anything!
When do you think I was at Princeton and Rockefeller?"
He bumps the table—whether deliberately or acciden-
tally is hard to tell—and my wife and I grab our drinks,
saving what we can. Mickey pays no attention. "I have
news for you. I never was. Never."

"I know."

"Yeah, you know everything. Well, let me remind
you when we last saw each other."

I wait, wondering if I've forgotten some important additional link. If he hadn't said "last," I'd think
maybe he was in kindergarten when I was in prekinder-
garten. Having said "last," I'd be sure it was at some
psychiatrist's office, if I went to a psychiatrist. Holding
on to my drink, I watch his eyes, wondering what chronological distortion lies behind them.

"Dr. Schwartz's, that's where."

I try to place Dr Schwartz. Is he a psychiatrist?
Then I remember. "The periodontist?"

"Yeah," Mickey snarls, "maybe three, four years
ago."

"I'm surprised. I thought you were too young for
periodontia."

"More of that Princeton/Rockefeller stuff? A
little joke? If I didn't respect old age, you'd never get out
of this restaurant alive." I glance at the silverware,
making sure I can reach it before Mickey can. He lowers
his voice. "Are you jealous? Is that it?" he asks, turning
suddenly without waiting for an answer and returning
to his table, arms still flapping.

"Well, that was a good idea," I tell my wife, "getting to know him. How many years do you think he knocked off his age?"

My wife looks over at their table and studies them again. "At least ten," she replies. "I'll say one thing, though—he lies with great conviction. Unless —" she studies me now—"unless you're lying."

A Dead Cousin

"Si died last night. In his sleep. Pam asked me to call."

Though my cousin Stephanie's delivery is brusque, shocked grief punctuates her words. It takes a moment to remember that, despite her being from the other side of my family, Mother's side, Stephanie has been closer to my cousin Simon than I have and closer also to his mother, my Aunt Pamela. After all, for years they've lived near one another in Greenwich Village, and Stephanie, in her early fifties, is—was!—the same age as Si, five years younger than me. I feel suddenly as if I'm no more than a neutral link between them—my living cousin on Mother's side and my dead cousin on Father's. Perhaps too neutral a link.

"Si and Pam were so close, so devoted to each other," I say finally. "I sometimes wondered how he would survive her death. I didn't think he could. But I never thought he'd die first."

"Yes," Stephanie replies, "she's eighty-five, and still getting around, doing her own shopping."

"Haven't seen either of them in over a year. Amy and I ran into them at theater. Not long after his heart attack. But he seemed to be doing fine. Courtly as ever. Leading Aunt Pamela to a draft-free corner of the lobby.

Lighting her cigarette before I could make a move. Getting us all drinks. Repeating lines she'd missed during the first act. He made me feel as if I'd never really taken care of my mother. Or Amy's."

"Your wife doesn't have much to complain about." Stephanie laughs, perhaps suggesting the difference between our situations—her poorly paid free-lance illustrating, done in a small Village apartment, and my job as Curator of Contemporary Art at the Metropolitan Museum, a few blocks from Amy's and my large old co-operative apartment, in which the walls are covered with paintings that have enhanced enormously in value, as much as the co-op itself. "Of course Si adored Pam. She was his best friend. But he was that way with all of us. Always attentive. Always generous. You can't imagine what it was like going out with him. I don't mean flowers or candy or carriage rides in Central Park. I mean the things he saw—light on a building at a certain time of day; the positions of store dummies in the corner of a window; the remains of a poster, torn so some word or image became ambiguous. He took things out of the air—elusive accidents—and gave them to you." Stephanie's voice is ambiguous too, happy and sad. "And the things he found —" She pauses, clears her throat, begins another catalogue: "Sometimes in junk shops and galleries. But mostly on the sidewalk. And in the gutter. Scraps—bits of hardware, machinery, furniture—what he used in the collages and constructions that he gave too, more often than he sold." She pauses again. "Si wanted to be loved. He was loved. By most of us. Well, I have other calls to make. We'll be at Campbell's Chapel tonight at seven. The funeral's tomorrow at ten. Perhaps you'll call your mother and brother. Remember me to them —and Amy."

The conversation echoes in my mind, distracts me from my work. I can accept Stephanie's being called by Aunt Pamela. Even though I'm a blood relative, even though in childhood I knew Aunt Pam so much better than Stephanie did, they, I repeat, have surely become closer. Stephanie's closeness to Si bothers me more. If the gap between his age and mine prevented closeness as children, it should have become meaningless as we grew older. Maybe the reason it didn't was because of my comparative success as a curator (with an eye good enough to make large profits occasionally on my own purchases) and his comparative failure as an artist. Not that, like Stephanie, he was an illustrator, limited by the most literal commissions. No, he attempted work that seemed more personally fashionable. Condescending? Well, if I had ever indicated any of this to Si—or to Stephanie—I could understand his remoteness; but I never did. I was cordial and encouraging. I went to his openings. And, eventually, having told the museum's Acquisitions Committee that Si was a cousin and that I would therefore abstain from voting, I recommended a sculpture of his. It was bought from funds devoted to purchasing work by "promising young artists," and it remains Si's only work in the collection of a major museum—still promising, even after his death.

Why, then, did Stephanie have to lecture to me so lengthily, so aggressively, on virtues I had presumably missed in Si and, implicitly, in his work—whole catalogues of virtues that were now interfering with the museum catalogues I was supposed to be working on? "He was loved. *By most of us,*" Stephanie had said so pointedly. But all of her words now seemed pointed. "I don't think *your wife* has much to complain about....*Remember me* to them —and Amy." All represented precise choices, of the same sort that Stephanie had made years ago by insisting on the use of her full first name instead of "Stephie" or "Steph" which everyone called her as a child.

I recall those days when Stephie was skinny and athletic, even acrobatic, with darting bright blue eyes, a tiny pug nose, and a head full of brilliant red curls, bouncing as she hopped from one relative's lap to the next. Her older sister, my contemporary, who died at college in a car accident, used to tease Stephie about having a crush on me, telling her, in the sophisticated lingo of 'thirties movies, "You're wasting your time. He's too old for you." I was about twelve. I wonder now if Stephie's—Stephanie's—childhood crush lingers and if it explains her coolness toward Amy. After almost half a century—early marriage, three daughters, bitter divorce—can she be jealous of Amy? Of our two sons? I'll probably never know. I surely don't know how to explain my own feelings about Stephanie's near-eulogy of Si. Am I jealous of the dead cousin I hardly knew, jealous of Stephanie's relationship to him, whatever it was?

I'm still asking myself these questions that evening as Amy and I walk to the funeral chapel. Then I ask her, "Did you and Stephanie ever fight?"

"Fight?"

"Argue. Have friction."

Amy thinks for a moment. "Not really. I was annoyed after her divorce. We must have had her over three or four times to meet bachelors we knew—straight ones. But Stephanie hardly paid attention to them, seemed more interested in you. And she never expressed appreciation. Had us over for one of those mop-up cocktail parties. That's all. Anyway, I never showed my irritation. I guess all that was around the time she took up with Si. We saw less of her then."

"Took up with him?"

"There was certainly something going on—maybe just a merging of the two sides of your family." Amy giggles. "Till then I always thought Si was gay."

"A bit gay, a bit straight—who knows? What about you and Si? Any fights?"

"You must think I spend my life picking fights. Fact is I avoid them." Amy concentrates again, lifting her head slightly, as if searching for memories among the tops of buildings in the sky. "I was annoyed with him too. That time we did the birthday party for your mother. About a year after your father died. You remember, Si arrived with that painter—Luddy something—and their girlfriends. Four of them. Plus Pam. And Buddy. And his girlfriend. Seven altogether. A whole troop. Pretty disproportionate at a party for fifty. And without even calling. I suppose if he had, I'd've said yes. But he didn't. That's the point. Not before. And not after. One of the things he had in common with Stephanie. And then—" Amy looks once more toward the sky—"that picture story in the *Times*—Brother Buddy must have set it up—about Si's house in the Village. All those shelves of Art Deco bronzes, walls of 'Greenies.' Well, you know the next time we saw Si, I told him how much that kind of thing means to me. I asked him to invite us, and he said he would, and he never did. Your brother's been there—of course he's another Village bachelor—but everyone has. Except us."

"He invited us to one of his New Year's Eve parties. We're always away over the holidays."

"There are fifty-one other weeks in the year," Amy replies emphatically as we arrive at the funeral chapel.

The reception room looks almost empty, despite about twenty people scattered in small groups. Si's older brother Buddy—real name, Karl, like mine and two other grandsons of our paternal grandfather—stands near the room's entrance receiving visitors. The dome of his shaved head glows above dark horn-rimmed glasses and somber gray pin-striped suit. The well-dressed brunette, whose elegantly manicured hand grips the crook of his left elbow, looks like an accessory to his perfectly tailored outfit as he introduces her to the couple ahead of Amy and me. And Buddy himself looks every inch the dapper, cosmopolitan newspaperman—the *Times*'s Washington or London Desk at least. It would be hard to guess he sells advertising for the paper, right here in New York.

As we wait, I glance around the room. Luddy, the painter who came to our apartment, is nearby with a different young woman—a new wife, I assume, noticing a wedding ring. Besides her, there are a few other young women I don't recognize, several of them crying. Both of the other Karls—one "Bobby," one "Billy"—are in the background. And, farther across the room, Stephanie is standing alongside Si's open coffin. I don't see my mother or brother or Aunt Pam anywhere.

"It was good of you to come, Amy—Karl —" Buddy kisses Amy, shakes my hand. "I don't think you've met Connie—my fiancée."

"I'm sorry we meet under these circumstances," I say to her, feeling that my words are as mechanical as Buddy's and trying to remember how many previous fiancées of his I've been introduced to. Surely at least a dozen, of whom he married five or six. "I haven't seen your mother. How's she bearing up?"

"Oh, she's doing fine. You know Pam—she's strong. But she decided to save her strength for tomorrow. She's home with Bertha, her maid. Bertha's absolutely devoted to her. Like one of the family."

Another couple and another girl have backed up behind us. Amy and I move on, nod to Luddy, and stop to greet Cousin Bobby and his wife. While we're talking to them, I can see Stephanie, still standing at Si's coffin, and I'm struck by how different she looks from the way I remember her as a child. Her concentration is so quiet, her hair so gray, hardly a trace of red left in it. I excuse myself and walk toward her, noticing the thinness of her face, the tightness of her skin drawn over the low bridge of her nose and cheek bones where tears have left tracks in her make-up. I pat her lightly on the shoulder, she turns, looks at me with wet eyes, hugs me hard.

"I can't believe it," Stephanie says. "I can't believe Si's dead. And I can't believe he looks so life-like." She stares at Si's face, and I follow her gaze, studying his features—broad brow, wide-set eyes, sharp straight nose, dark mustache, cleft chin—all still strong, steel-gray, an amalgam of metal and wax, no more life-like than his sensitive hands folded rigidly over the lapels of a soft-looking navy-blue suit, perhaps cashmere. Only Stephanie can be bringing him, giving him, the life she sees. As her eyes dart over the coffin, I wonder if she isn't planning a portrait, sketching it now in her mind—the quarter of Si visible above the closed part of the coffin, covered with flowers. "Not really handsome," Stephanie whispers—perhaps to herself, perhaps to him, perhaps to me. "Not like a movie star. But he wanted to be handsome." She raises her voice slightly. "He made us see that he wanted to be. We responded to that—his want. " For the first time since I've been with her, Stephanie looks around the room, seeming to focus on some of the young women, then some of the men, seated and standing there. "They didn't necessarily love him—not all of them, not those boys either—but they loved his wanting them. He was seductive. You look like him. You're even better looking," she says, finally addressing me directly, "but you don't have *that*."

I pat her again on the shoulder, take her arm, and lead her away from the coffin just as my mother and brother come toward us.

"Pam's not here!" Mother begins as soon as she's kissed us. "Si was her life, her life. It's a terrible thing to say, but everyone knows that if she'd had the choice –" My brother looks hard at her as she looks at Buddy, still near the entrance; and she stops for a moment, then lowers her voice, "Well it's true—it's not that she can't face Si's being dead—there was enough warning when he had his heart attack—it's that she can't face Buddy still being alive when Si isn't. Buddy! I spoke to her just a day before Si's death. It was the same as always—Si, Si, Si. She hardly mentioned Buddy, and then only to say that the three of them were having dinner at Si's the next night. She told me it would be the first time in several months she'd be seeing Buddy and that he hadn't seen Si for even longer." Mother turns to Stephanie. "Isn't that right? You know about them. You see them."

Stephanie hesitates. "I don't know much about Buddy, but—yes, they all had dinner the night Si died."

"See!" Mother says. "And then this happened."

"Mother!" My brother stops her again. "You don't know what you're saying. I'm not sure I know."

"Well, I do. I'm saying Pam should be here. That's what I'm saying."

"You shouldn't —"

My brother starts to speak, but I interrupt him: "Buddy told me she's with Bertha, that she's saving her strength."

"With Bertha! She should be with us. That's what families are for. Times like this. We can give Pam our strength." Mother pauses. "Bertha! Her bargain! Pam's bragged enough about how little she pays her."

Amy and I meet Bertha the next morning in the reception room. Though it's crowded now with members of the family, remaining until the funeral starts, and with a continually changing group of Si's friends and colleagues, passing through on their way to the chapel, Bertha's presence is powerful. A huge calm black woman, perhaps double the size of Aunt Pam and thirty years younger, she guards the unoccupied end of the couch on which they sit, with Pam propped between her and the arm. The contrast between Bertha's dark bulk and Pam's pale frailty is startling.

Pam looks at me from tearful eyes sunken in purplish rings. "It's been hard, Karl, so hard, harder even than when your Uncle Max died. He married late— we were together for less than thirty years—but at least he had a full life, bless him. With Si there was hardly a day in his entire life I didn't see him or speak to him. His entire life! Fifty-two years! Nothing!"

"I understand," I mutter feebly while Bertha's large muscular arm hugs and supports Pam.

"You can't. You can't possibly," Pam sobs. "You're an older brother. It's not the same. Si was my baby, my baby."

"Mine too," Bertha says, continuing to hug Pam. "He was such a good child, such a good son, so—giving."

The funeral director asks the family to take seats in the chapel. Bertha lifts Pam to her feet and holds one of her arms while I take the other.

"Get Buddy," I whisper to Amy, glancing at him on the other side of the room, where, as during the previous evening, he's greeting people and introducing his fiancée.

"Now, that boy's never where you want him," Bertha tells me, talking across Pam, as Amy leaves. I wonder if, perhaps like Pam, where Bertha really wants Buddy is in Si's coffin.

Still holding Connie on his arm, Buddy meets us at the chapel entrance and awkwardly replaces me at Pam's side. Dropping back and rejoining Amy, I watch him try to take Connie, Pam, and Bertha, four abreast, through the entrance. At last, he unlocks arms with Connie, and he and Bertha lead Pam to the front pew, followed by Connie. They have barely sat down before Buddy gets them on their feet again to make room for Connie on his left. Amy and I wait for my mother and brother, then take seats in the next row.

"The first seat," Mother whispers, pointing at Connie's back. "Is she part of the family?"

"Soon to be," my brother replies, lifting his finger to his lips.

"I'll speak briefly," the minister begins, "as is befitting a life cut so short... a life snuffed out like a candle burning brilliantly... an unmaterialistic life devoted to

his art, still glowing, still with us... public accomplish-
ment insufficiently recognized but private devotion to
mother, brother and friends recognized by all who knew
him..." The minister emphasizes these phrases, recites
the Twenty-third Psalm, then introduces "Simon's lov-
ing brother Karl."

Buddy stands, removes his glasses, places them
carefully behind the handkerchief in his breast pocket,
takes a deep breath. "There are brothers, and there are
close brothers. Si and I were close, so close we hardly had
to see one another to know what each was doing. When
Si was happy, I was happy. When Si was sad, I was sad.
When Si was sick, I was sick. And I know that the
converse was also true. Si gave his thoughts and feelings
to me again and again throughout his life. He always
phoned at the right time when I was at college, wrote at
the right time when I was in the army, never forgot my
birthday or anniversary—anniversaries." Buddy sup-
presses a smile, pauses, reaches up to wipe the lenses of
his glasses he forgets he has removed. "I was privileged
to spend the last evening of Si's life with him and our
dear mother. Typically, we had not seen each other in a
while. Just as typically, that made no difference. We took
up from where we'd left off—or, more accurately, from
where we had never left off, not since childhood."

Buddy sits down, and there's a long pause before
the minister introduces , "Ludwig Mueller, Simon's
closest friend." During that pause, I remember Mother's
words—"*See! And then this happened.*"—and I wonder
now just what, if anything, happened earlier, at that final
dinner. Could nothing happening—nothing, as usual,
between Buddy and Si, Buddy and Pam—have killed Si?

Those of us in the front pews turn as Luddy rises
and begins to speak.

"It wouldn't surprise me," his voice trembles, "if many of you here think you were Si's closest friend. Certainly many of you think he was your closest friend. Yes, he was one of those people who had many closest friends. He gave so much of himself, his art, his hospitality. Some of you have a key to his house, but you rarely needed it. His door was open. His heart was open. You were always welcome. There was always food and drink and a place to stay. There was always room on his walls for the work of other artists. I think sometimes that Si put more of his energy into being a host than being an artist. He was the one who had friends back after openings. His life seemed to be a continuous party. It was appropriate that the year ended as it began, with his New Year's Eve bash, larger and larger each year. I hate to think of future New Year's Eves. They could be nights of gloom, unless we all remember that Si wouldn't have wanted it that way. He would have wanted us to have a good time. And he can remain with us, hiding inside unknown bartenders, filling our glasses—for toasts to him."

Luddy's words, still trembling and mixed now with the sound of sobs and sniffles, hang over us as he sinks into his seat and the minister announces that the family will receive at Si's house after the interment.

"Well!" Mother says, her eyes following the procession led by Bertha from the front pew. "I believed him—he spoke like a friend, was a friend—but not Buddy. He must have worked awfully hard on his speech. 'Never left off, not since childhood!' They used to fight like cats and dogs. Pam was always afraid they'd kill each other."

"How could Si afford to do so much entertaining?" I ask, returning to Luddy's eulogy.

Mother squints. Her expression becomes shrewd. "Pam told me that Mueller was very good to Si too. These things don't work one way. His father's Victor Mueller, one of the most successful men on Wall Street. They took care of Si's investments."

"Si also sold a few paintings, just like you," my brother adds. "There was a sort of standing joke. Whenever he did anything extravagant, everyone would say, 'Well, another blank spot on the wall.' He was very decent. Never sold a picture by a living artist. And the blank spots filled up quickly, usually with the work of younger artists."

I turn to Amy. "A moral dilemma, isn't it?"

"Selling the work of a living artist? You've never done that."

"No, I meant going to Si's house. The way you feel about him," I continue to tease her. "Never had us there when he was alive."

"No dilemma, moral or otherwise," Amy replies, smiling. "I want to see those Greenies."

Pam and Bertha, Connie and Buddy, and my mother and brother leave the cemetery in the first limousine. Amy and I, the Muellers, Stephanie and another neighbor of Pam's follow in the next car. The neighbor talks almost all the way to the Village.

"There's no justice," she begins, "none at all. A death like Si's makes one question God's existence—His judgment at least. How could He take Si from Pam? Si was all she had. He and Bertha. And he made Bertha possible—he's been supplementing her salary for years, gives her an extra hundred dollars a week. One of you should speak to Buddy and be sure he continues that."

"If he doesn't, I will," Luddy says.

"Well, you shouldn't have to," the neighbor goes on. "I understand Si left almost everything to Buddy—the house and everything in it. What will Buddy do with all that? Sell it? He's an uptown type and, anyway, he doesn't understand what Si collected. Pam thinks the whole thing—the building as is—has to be worth millions in today's market. But, say, one—one million. Pam could've used that and doled out what she wanted to Buddy. And think of all Si's friends—artists mostly—think how they could've used the money. It makes me sick." She pauses briefly. "Even with Bertha, what life will Pam have? She had dinner with Si two or three times a week. She went to his parties. She shared his friends. Who'll amuse her now? Bertha? Buddy?"

"We—" Luddy's wife starts.

"I know. You'll look in occasionally. So will I. And Stephanie. But that's not like going out, going to Si's. The way he cooked. And the place itself. Like a museum. Pam always said his collecting was a kind of giving, that he wanted to share what he liked, the things on his walls. But all of you know that."

"We've never been there," Amy says.

"Odd," the neighbor replies. "He loved people, loved to show his things. I can't imagine that house empty. Or done over by a new owner ...."

By the time we arrive at Sullivan Street I'm fed up with Si's generosity, the generosity that won or bought so many friends, the generosity he never wasted on Amy and me. However, I no longer think that the reason has anything to do with our respective economic situations. Obviously he was as well off as I am, maybe better off. I look for other reasons—downtown versus uptown, bohemia versus the bourgeoisie, artist versus curator—but all of these seem too simple, too reductive. And yet *I'm* thinking in these categories, not Si, not generous Si. I wonder if sometime in our years of intermittent contact I may have made a disparaging remark to him about the Village, rebellious dress, or maybe artists in general. All seem unlikely. Before moving to our present place, Amy and I lived happily in the Village. And Si was always a bit of a dandy; like his brother he loved good suits, the kind he was buried in. As to "artists in general," I've written again and again, in articles and catalogue introductions, that the category doesn't exist, that there are only individual artists.

The house is a three-story former loft building, about twenty-five feet wide. A garage or truck berth occupies most of the ground floor and, alongside its large closed overhead doors, there's a much smaller entrance with its door open. We enter a vestibule leading to a steep staircase that Pam's neighbor and the Muellers begin to climb. Stephanie lingers to show us things she thinks we might otherwise miss.

"He had such a good sense of humor," she says, pointing at a mounted bronze-framed lobby directory containing the names of many firms and individuals. "He found that at a demolition site in the Wall Street area. And those"— she points toward the opposite wall, at a row of odd-shaped hat blocks on a long shelf—"a women's hat factory near here went out of business. He bought the whole lot, gave most of the blocks to friends, just kept enough to use as hat racks. At one time he had maybe a hundred straw hats stacked here—you know, old fashioned boaters with striped bands—gave them away too. He used to say, 'That's what art's all about—

finding things: the world exists at your feet—and in the classified section of the *Times*.'" For the first time with us during the past two days, Stephanie begins to laugh, then stifles the impulse. "Of course he used most of what he found—in his art. Well—" she points upstairs.

On the way up we pass dozens of posters, prints, store signs, masks, flags, pennants, hunks of ornamental moulding and sculpture from demolished buildings .... From antique handrail to pressed-tin ceiling, there's hardly any wall space. Many steps before we reach the landing, above which a ship's prow head looms, I'm questioning, questioning with each step, the minister's phrase about Si's "unmaterialistic life."

The stairwell walls seem empty compared with those on the second floor. Here they're covered all the way from the floor to the ceiling. Behind a free-standing kitchen counter, obviously once a commercial bar, the collection of Greenies is placed on shelves running half the length of the room. Amy gasps at this parade of highly stylized, almost sexless bronze sculptures patinated in a forest-like range of greens—elegant nudes; thinly veiled dancing girls; yesteryear's bathing beauties in suits with elbow-length sleeves and knee-length pants; other sleek, muscleless "athletes," male as well as female, dressed for tennis, golf, and horseback riding; some men holding women in chaste, balletic embraces— all a fantasy world of playthings and playmates; all, I'm beginning to think, an extension of my dead cousin. Or is it the other way around? Is Si the extension—part of his own collection?

"Not high art," Stephanie says, perhaps noticing both Amy's excitement and my impatience, "but still wonderful, aren't they? And his Frosties."

She leads us to a cabinet full of grainy white, thirties lamps in the shapes of airplanes, balloons, zeppelins, and parachutes, poised on chrome bases. I glance from the cabinet to a large Victorian couch across the room where Pam and Bertha and my mother and brother are seated at right angles to the Muellers and Pam's neighbor on a smaller matching settee. They are surrounded by younger men and women, many of whom were not at the cemetery.

"He had so many fans," Stephanie continues, looking at a tall, short-haired brunette who waves to her and comes toward us.

The woman, maybe thirty, is broad-shouldered, almost hipless, a living Greenie. She walks across the room in long strides, kisses Stephanie on the mouth, then introduces herself before Stephanie can. "Mike," she says, offering a large hand to Amy and me, then resting it on Stephanie's shoulder, and talking to her. "It's almost like New Year's Eve, isn't it? Except—"

"Yes, *except.*"

Amy and I excuse ourselves to join Pam's group. On the way, I wonder if Mike is short for Michelle and if, to her, Stephanie is Steve. Once again I feel rather uneasily possessive of Stephanie and now a bit jealous of Mike as well as Si.

"Have you seen it all?" Pam's neighbor asks Amy. "Have you been upstairs? And down to the studio?"

"No," Amy replies, "we're just starting."

I look past the neighbor at a wall full of pictures— two by Si, most by better known artists, several by painters unknown to me. The works hang close together above equally crowded bookshelves in which I recognize a few of my monographs. "It would take a long time to go through everything here."

"A long time!" Pam is offended. "A lifetime, you mean. Si put his life into this place. Amy's right. You're just starting. You haven't begun."

"Well, it's not the Metropolitan Museum," Mother replies, coming to my defense.

Bertha pats Pam's arm, trying to calm her. "I'd hate to have to clean here."

"There's a good place to start your tour," the neighbor says, indicating the south end of the floor, filled with exotic plants in majolica pots standing among life-size pieces of cast-stone garden sculpture.

We duck beneath palms, philodendrons, ficus and bamboo, making our way past statues of dwarfs and giants—cupids, Bacchus, Diana, Hercules—all looking as gray-green and lifeless as Si did yesterday. "It's eerie," Amy remarks. "Let's go upstairs."

Again the stair walls are loaded, though less randomly now. On one side, there's a large group of pornographic Japanese wood-block prints; on the other, several of Matisse's odalisques and Picasso's late erotic etchings.

"Well," Amy sighs with relief, "at least these look alive. Larger than life," she adds, giggling.

"Aren't you glad now you weren't here when Si was? You'd never have felt free to stare like this."

"I'm not staring. Picasso is."

Si's bedroom, about twenty-five feet square, occupies this end of the third floor. It's a large room with no room in it. Above a double bed, covered by overlapping quilts, there's a collection of Kachina dolls, commemorating a winter in New Mexico. At the foot of the bed a large Italianate table supports dozens of Mickey Mouse toys. An open Pennsylvania Dutch pie cabinet in the left corner of the room is filled with scrimshaw and macramé. Another, in the right corner, contains bowls and baskets, ships and houses, made of bottle caps. There are smaller tables covered with netsuke, snuff boxes, glass paperweights, souvenirs of the 1939 World's Fair. Above everything hangs a bronze chandelier shaped like a flock of bats with wings touching. Each bat holds an electric light between feet that grip like tiny hands.

"Did I say eerie?" Amy asks. "The word's not strong enough."

We peek into Si's bathroom, fitted with solid brass plumbing and white porcelain fixtures bearing the name of an Edinburgh manufacturer. Barely glancing at the photographs there of movie stars, nudes, Greek and Indian sculpture, we hurry on to the next bedroom. As we approach, we hear a woman ask, "How can anyone know what this junk is worth?"

"There are professionals—appraisers, auctioneers," Buddy answers as we enter the room. "Hi, Amy. Hi, Karl. Connie and I were just talking about these things—their delightful eccentricity." He gestures as if grabbing everything from the walls and other surfaces. "Si called this room The Cigar Box. You see, each piece is decorated with cigar bands or made from cigar boxes or match sticks. Even the bed. Can you imagine how many hours that took? A lot of it is what he called tramp-art or prison-art. Trouble is that's all I know, what he told us. Would there be anyone at the museum who could tell us, maybe give us an idea, of what this stuff's worth?"

"The museum has rules against giving appraisals, but I can get you the name of a qualified expert." I stop, as when editing a catalogue. "Redundant!" Buddy looks puzzled. "Qualified expert. Expert will do."

"Oh! Thanks. Call me at the *Times*." He sounds as if he wants to hire me.

Amy and I hurry on to a room filled with Belter furniture carved in convoluted floral patterns and illuminated by Tiffany lamps seemingly grown in the same lush aesthetic garden.

"The more I see, the less I know," I tell Amy. "About Si, I mean."

"Yes, the Greenies were enough."

"Nothing's enough," I reply, leading her to the next room in this maze of collections within the overall collection.

This room looks like a Hollywood set from the thirties—polar bear rug, sleek white lacquer, chrome. As we enter, Stephanie and Mike rise from a satin chaise longue tucked in the corner behind the door.

"Isn't it something?" Stephanie asks, straightening her dress. "Every time I come here, to this house, it's like having a choice of dreams. Have you seen The Cigar Box?" Amy and I nod. "And the Stickley Room? And the Fifties Modern?" We shake our heads. "There's so much to digest."

"Digestion was never the point." Mike's tongue darts between slightly smeared lips. "It's about pleasure, shared pleasure."

Amy and I visit the rooms we haven't seen, then return to the stair and go down to Si's studio in the former garage. There, amidst a clutter representing every ism of Twentieth Century art, every phase of Si's work, Luddy is talking to a group of artists surrounding a table at the center of the floor.

"... the piece he was working on when he died," Luddy tells them. "Such a shame. He was just entering this new period—welding."

We walk around the table, studying an abstract construction made of bolts and gears and steel plates, then continue to the far end of the studio. A shallow raised open nook that must once have been a loading platform contains Si's desk and chair and, opposite them, a cot built into a wall of bookcases. On the shelves and the desk wall are many photographs. A nude baby-picture of Si, buttocks up, face grinning toothlessly at the camera. A recent parody of the same shot, taken of Si on the bearskin rug Amy and I have just seen. Luddy and Si and my brother in sailors' uniforms during the Korean War. The famous photograph of Jackson Pollock sitting on the running board of his Model-A Ford, and one of David Smith in a welding mask, and others of artists Si admired, artists who, in effect, gave him permission to do his work. Young women, dozens of them, dressed and undressed. Stephanie, older than the rest, wearing a false mustache and comical party hat. Pam at every age. Pam as a beautiful child with dark wide-open eyes peering from under equally dark straight hair. Pam as an exquisite bride, whose lacy white veil and clear pale skin contrast with her hair, her eyes, the dim cavities of her finely formed nostrils, and the long shadow of her elegant neck. Pam just married to my Uncle Max, already stooped, gray, and bald, wearing thick-lensed glasses. I identify him for Amy.

"They're almost grotesque," she says. "As a couple."

"Max was a nice man, a successful lawyer. The way my father told it, the family didn't think anyone was good enough for Pam—handsome enough, rich enough. She refused several men closer to her own age. Must have been in her early twenties—old to be single then—

when Max came along. She may have been older still. Father probably knocked off a couple of years."

As I study this picture and then some others—one of Buddy and Si, in shorts, holding hands; another of a family party at which Father, looking as much like Si as me, stands with his arm protectively around Pam's shoulders—I wonder if this photographic information, these black-and-white facts mean more, tell more about Si, than the hundreds of things stuffed into his house. Will they be sold as a lot, along with everything else? Stephanie spoke of torn posters, ambiguous words and images. Now all of life and death, this entire house, seems like a torn poster. Everything is ambiguous. Si's sexuality—and Stephanie's. Si's generosity. Si's friends. Si's art. Si's investments.

I look down from the platform at Luddy, still talking about Si's work. His stance, his gestures are those of a lecturer, just as those of the young people listening to him are those of students. Stephanie spoke too of store dummies in random positions. That's the way everyone looks now, as if locked in some temporary pose. One of the young men in the circle around Luddy looks up at Amy and me. I can imagine what he sees: middle-aged, middle-class mannequins. Tourists in an artist's studio, straights, breeders.... For a moment I feel disoriented, as if between mirrors, as if both inside and outside. Then I remember where I am and know I want to leave.

Upstairs, Buddy and Connie have joined the group with Pam.

"Your brother deserves more than a paid funeral announcement," Pam's telling Buddy. "I want him to have a real obituary."

"I'm trying," he replies. "I need more information—the dates of Si's exhibitions, the collections he's in. Luddy was supposed to—"

"Luddy's done enough." Pam points at the drinks and platters of food on the bar. "Everything you need is in the studio—Si's catalogues, his scrapbooks. And while you're there, check the locks. They should be changed. I don't want anything walking off."

As Buddy starts to lead Connie to the back stair, he says to me, "You won't forget that call?"

My brother takes me aside. "There are a few boys here I want to talk to," he whispers. "Haven't seen them since New Year's Eve. Will you and Amy take Mother uptown?"

"Of course," I reply, wondering why he asked. Mother's on our way; and I understand, am too often like now, made to understand, that he spends more time with her, does more for her, than I do.

Amy and I say good-bye to him and the others, leave Si's house, and find a cab.

"I'll sit in the middle," Mother says, wanting to be cushioned against bumps and potholes. "Karl, tell the driver there's no hurry," she adds, plenty loud enough for him to hear. "The locks aren't all that will be changed!" she resumes, rocking between us, and feeling lighter and frailer than she sounds. "Pam's amazing, thinking of that at a time like this. Buddy's the one who should've thought of it. If he wasn't so busy thinking about that vacant fiancée. Between the two of them, they don't have a brain in their heads. And the obituary too. Not that Si's not dead without it. But still, Pam's right, there should be some record, some public recognition. I hope you'll take better care of your younger brother." Mother pauses, realizing what she's said. "Of course, finally, it was Si who took care of Buddy. Good care." She pauses again. "Well, I don't want anything. Just to be buried and left in peace. Your brother and you two and your boys are the only obituary I need. How are the children?"

Amy carefully and selectively recounts their most recent accomplishments, then returns to the original subject. "The only thing missing at Si's was a collection of armor."

"I told Pam it wasn't the Metropolitan," Mother says.

I question Amy's observation. To me, now, that's just what Si's place seems—a vast collection of armor—everything there, including his most recent work. Everything, hiding and revealing him, protecting and imprisoning him. More than the Greenies, Si himself is still the centerpiece of his own collection. Si! And Pam! Pam, wearing a helmet and carrying a shield. Pam, the other fixed point in this elliptical orbit.

At Mother's apartment house, as I help her out of the cab and walk her to the door, I'm aware again of how light she feels. Does she weigh as little as Pam? When she's with my brother, is she heavier on his arm than on mine?

I return to the cab, give our address to the driver, and begin thinking about Amy's and my apartment. What would anyone make of the art and furnishings there? From these things and from my own publications—things, also, neatly arranged on shelves in my study—from this evidence, less generous than what Si left behind, what would people think? What would they know? And would it be more or less than when I was alive?

Questions. Questions breeding more questions. And none answered. Perhaps I, too, will have a last dinner with my mother and brother. Perhaps they and Amy and our sons will sit staring at the things on our walls, no one saying anything—nothing killing, anyway.

After several blocks, blocks of silence, Amy remarks, "You look gloomy. I didn't know Si meant that much to you."

"I feel as if—as if I'm already someone's dead cousin, as if all of us are."

Search

Something, someone must be chasing them. They keep moving from neighborhood to neighborhood, then from place to place within the same neighborhood, seeking some small island within the island of Manhattan itself, some tiny, protected, peaceful, comfortable spot, no more than a dot on a grid, a pinpoint beside a drop of water or a pock of park.

They go from the Hudson to the East River, from uptown to downtown, from low floors to high, wanting another view, more or less space, better service.

External factors hardly matter — at first, an enlarging family; later, one that shrinks as their children go off on their own. Somewhere, they know, there's the place of their dreams. Perhaps a penthouse from which they can see both rivers and can touch the sky. Or a maisonette where they can walk straight in, greeting no one, neither doorman nor elevator operator; an apartment like a house, at sidewalk level, guarded by a lonely tree that casts an almost human shadow. Or one on a compromise floor, floating between clouds and concrete — maybe the seventh, maybe the thirteenth — a height from which they'll move eventually, up or down.

The changing size of their family, the wife's need for a new neighborhood, the husband's relocated office (he prefers to walk to work) — all these are only excuses to move. Both of them want to smell fresh paint. Both want to see their things against a different background in a different setting.

Real estate brokers, architects, movers answer their calls for help. For the moment the undertaker's line is busy.

The Couch

The large black horsehair sofa, with red buttons between its tufts, was my favorite piece of furniture even when I was a girl growing up in our brownstone. Before I was allowed to play in the living room, and before I realized that four arms dropped from the sofa's back to form five seats, and long before I understood the word "Victorian," this single piece—opposite the basalt mantel, complementing its darkness, and occupying so much of the high parlor floor's main wall—was the hub of all the smaller, sleeker, skinny-legged furniture that fanned out from it. Later, when I could climb up onto the couch, I loved to creep under its arms and, still later, to ride them, bouncing as actively as the flames in the fireplace across the room.

"Be careful," Mother said, stroking one of the couch's arms, lovingly, possessively. "The horsehair's old. I've had the upholsterer. All he can do is repairs. You can't get this material anymore. It's like iron, made to last —except when six-year-olds bounce on it."

"Horsehair?" My eyes must have opened wide— bright and round as the couch's buttons.

"Yes, real horsehair. They used to take it from the mane or the tail."

Mother didn't need to say more. The fabric—hard, smooth, shiny in spots—was special. As I climbed down from the arm, crawling over tufts and buttons toward Mother's lap, I could smell horses, a whole stableful.

"Where'd you find it?" I asked, knowing by then that my parents spent Saturdays in antique shops, finding things.

"It came with the house. The couple we bought it from couldn't use it. They were moving to an apartment."

Apartments were where most of my friends lived. Usually smaller than houses, they had no room for a couch like this—made from a horse, and as large as one.

Several years later, Father recalled buying the house. "That was just before you were born. We were a bit apart on price. I didn't want to dicker. Mommy loved the couch, had to have it. I said, throw it in, and it's a deal."

"It's very old, isn't it?" I asked, sniffing once again between its musty tufts.

"No," Father replied. "That was the surprise. The sellers must have thought I thought the couch was extremely valuable. They explained—carefully, honestly—that it was made in the late 'thirties. By a German refugee who could design anything—homes, offices, industrial products, stage sets. He'd been at the Bauhaus." Father pointed at some of the bright, thin-legged furniture. "But they told him they liked Victorian, and he gave them that. What they wanted—something big and fanciful—the way he would have for a Broadway show. He was famous once. Now, I don't even remember his name. Haven't heard it in years. I wonder if he's still alive."

I could hardly follow Father. He finished with a sigh. I sighed back, understanding only that the couch had a history and, again, that it was too big for an apartment.

But, still later, when Father left his investment firm to work at home as a consultant, he explained suddenly that now he needed an apartment, needed services that weren't possible in the house—a doorman to announce visitors, someone to receive mail and other deliveries.

"We could put in an elevator," Mother said, willing to accept necessary surgery on the house she loved.

"I don't want to spend my life going up and down. I do enough of that—on graph paper."

Father's joke, like some of his graphs, fell flat.

"An announcer system at the front door—" Mother tried again, suggesting a minor operation this time.

"No!" Father's voice was emphatic, harsh and bullying. "What I want is one level instead of four ... a handyman when something needs fixing ... "

Like Mother, I knew that he could have gone on and on, that his threat to move was as final as if he had finished his list of reasons for doing so.

After months of talk and searching, my parents found a rambling apartment in a building from the days of large families. It had five bedrooms—one for themselves; one for me; one for my brother who was away at college; and two to be used as offices by Father and his secretary.

"The couch is too big for this living room," Father observed as he studied the plan of the new apartment. "There wouldn't be room for anything else."

Mother got the tape measure. "It's not quite ten feet," she said. "We could use it in the front hall. We'll need a place to drop things, to put on galoshes, whatever."

"It's not like a ten-foot pencil line on a wall. It has bulk." Father took the tape from her. "Over three feet deep. That's almost half the hall, a third, anyway. Wouldn't a small table and chair do just as well?"

"Do? Functionally, you mean? Like in a waiting room? You'll never see another couch like this. It's one of a kind—German ingenuity wedded to British whimsy." Mother smiled, pleased with her description.

"German weight added to Victorian excess," Father amended her.

I listened to them bicker, rooting for Mother, while intuitively understanding that their differences—Father's cool efficiency, Mother's sentimental attachment to things—were like parts in a play they enjoyed re-enacting, and that the couch was simply a prop in the same play. And I guessed that Father actually enjoyed indulging Mother, and indirectly himself, in expressions of impracticality forbidden to him in his world of investment counseling.

The couch had to be brought up on top of the elevator. The front door of the apartment was removed from the buck to allow clearance into the foyer. Once there, I felt it was there forever—a large dark refuge.

While still in the lower grades, my friends and I sat there sometimes, in a line, giggling and pretending to be in the back of the school bus. Mostly, though, the couch was used, as Mother said it would be, for coats and packages and, in bad weather, for taking off wet shoes or putting on rubbers. At first, Father made jokes about "outsize functionalism... overkill... using a man to do a boy's job," but gradually he seemed to accept the couch in its new location, referring to it gently, even affectionately, as "an artifact of our past life."

During my high school years, I was surely the only member of our family who, for no apparent reason, no functional need, sometimes dropped a pair of the couch's arms and sat cuddling between them, arms on arms in mutual embrace, remembering the fireplace I'd known as a child. I was almost able to see it, projected from my mind onto the flickering foyer wall where it remained mine, unshared with the family that now occupied the brownstone and enjoyed the real basalt thing, an almost immovable "artifact." Recalling Father's word, I also recalled its use by a teacher while lecturing on a much more distant past in front of a mummy in its case at the museum. I suspected that the fabric surrounding the mummy, like the horsehair surrounding me, must have a similar odor of antiquity, the smell of stallions drawing celestial chariots and barges.

My brother moved out of the apartment during my sophomore year at college. By spring recess of senior year I, too, was planning to leave.

"I'm used to more freedom, more privacy," I told my parents.

"In a dormitory!" Mother replied.

"They're not like when you went to college. You've told me about your days—checking in and out. It isn't like that." I watched mother's eyes become slightly wet, as if to put out the fiery irritation behind them. I rushed on. "I want to go to Europe this summer. Then get a job and an apartment."

"That's a lot all at once," Father said. "You'll lose a year. If you're determined to travel, why not stay in this apartment till after you find a job?"

I was surprised by Father's matter-of-fact tone. His eyes were dry.

"With your brother gone and you leaving," he continued, "we'll want a smaller place. The maintenance has gone way up, and I'm not as busy as I was." He paused. "If you're patient, there'll be enough things here to furnish your place."

My eyes swept through the living room, the foyer, and beyond, removing furniture from the floor, bric-a-brac from the shelves, pictures from the walls, chandeliers from the ceiling. "How much smaller will the new apartment be?"

"I'm not sure. At least two rooms, yours and your brother's. Maybe three. Maybe four. We don't really need a full dining room. I may be able to work with a part-time secretary in my office. It all depends on room size, layout."

My eyes came to rest on the couch in the foyer. Pointing, I said, "Then you won't want that?"

"Probably not," Father replied quickly, eagerly.

His words were barely out, still hanging in the air like the chandeliers I'd glanced at, when Mother, raising her voice slightly, said, "Wait. You said it depends on layout. We haven't found an apartment yet. Neither has she. Who knows what we'll want, what she'll want? Maybe we can use that couch. Maybe the daybed in her brother's room will fit better in her new place. Some of his other things too. There are a lot of maybes."

"A lot in your mind." Father looked annoyed, sounded annoyed, but his voice softened somewhat as he patted Mother's hair, in much the same way he had often patted mine, and said, "I don't know what's going on in there, in that lovely head of yours. I'm not eager to move—I remember last time—but, if we do, there are no maybes about what I want. I want to make some money on this apartment, and I want to reduce our maintenance. In the kind of apartment I'm thinking of, there won't be room for that couch."

"You can't tell," Mother insisted. "I wish I had a mind like yours. I wish I thought I could see into the future. But no one can. Not even you."

I listened to them, watched them, feeling uncomfortable, different from the way I felt on the couch, in it. "How long will it take to find another apartment?"

"Finding it's only the beginning." Father looked at me, then up at the ceiling, as I'd seen him do frequently with charts and graphs and sheets of figures. "We have to sell this place, find another, fix it up. My guess is the end of the year." He paused, turning to Mother. "What d'you think, dear?"

"I don't want to think about it. I'm not like you and your son. I can't just abandon everything."

I returned from Europe in the fall, eager to see the new apartment my parents had described in letters, and more eager still to find a place of my own.

"You're going to be shocked," Father said. "The price of co-ops has gone through the roof. Rents too. I'll help all I can, but I still think you should find a job first, then look for an apartment. At least you'll know what you can afford."

"I only need a room. When can I see your new place?"

Mother replied, "That's easy. I'm going there tomorrow. Have to check on a few things—paint colors, kitchen details."

The new apartment was much smaller than the old one; much, much smaller than the house I still remembered well. Mother and I walked through quickly, barely stopping in the living room; dining alcove; and master bedroom, which Father would use as an office to be shared with his secretary. In the second bedroom painters were already priming the walls. Mother stopped for a moment to approve color samples, then led me to the kitchen where a plumber, an electrician, and a carpenter were conferring with the decorator. While Mother resolved the location of the sink counter and cabinets and lighting above it, I peeked into a maid's room behind the kitchen before returning to the living room. I was standing at the window there, looking down at Central Park, when Mother joined me.

"Yes," she said, putting her arm around my shoulder, "that's what we're paying for, the view. It's the only thing here that has any feeling of space. Well, you see we won't need most of the furniture we have."

"The couch?"

Mother turned and pointed at the main living room wall, opposite the fireplace. "It would be like old times."

I smiled. "Not if you want anything else in the room."

"You sound like your father. He's convinced it won't work. He's even got our decorator convinced."

"Wouldn't it make more sense to use the two small couches on either side of the fireplace?"

"Your father has been coaching you, hasn't he? Tell me the truth."

"No. I give you my word."

At lunch he asked me how I liked the apartment.

"I was surprised. It's really tiny."

"Fact of life—expansion and contraction. We don't need much space. When your mother's through, it'll be cozy."

"You won't let me make it cozy," Mother replied. "It's pieces like the couch—"

"You're confusing cozy and crowded."

The couch continued to come up in their conversations, while I looked for a job and an apartment. Every morning I studied the newspaper, turning quickly past the big stories to the tiny ones—column inches of HELP WANTED and APARTMENTS AVAILABLE.

"It's hopeless," I told my parents again and again, week after week. "I went to see a so-called studio apartment with cathedral ceiling. What that meant was a room, closet-kitchen, and bath, in a five-story walk up; ceiling about eight feet, except for a small skylight a couple of feet higher. The other windows were blocked by a fire escape. I was wondering which route the burglars would choose, when the agent said the place was a bargain."

"You'll do better than that," Father assured me. "What about the job situation?"

"The usual: I don't have enough experience. I don't type fast enough. I'm not computer literate."

"You should brush up on your typing. The secretarial schools give word processing too."

Three more weeks went by before, one night after dinner, I announced, "I guess I won't get what I want without typing. So I'm going to concentrate on that—and an apartment. I saw a nice three today. Only one problem. It cost too much."

"Maybe you could share with one of your friends," Mother suggested.

"Mother! I'm used to a room of my own. I'm —" I stopped, realizing I sounded spoiled.

Father studied the living room ceiling. "Even sharing would be expensive—unless you have a good job."

"Don't worry. I'll get one, a good one."

I looked at the couch, wanting, if I'd been alone, to sit there in the one piece of furniture that offered true comfort and security. When I went to my room, I felt crowded, remembering how the brownstone of my childhood had been compressed into this apartment, and imagining how this one would be still further compressed into the next. I tried to trace the history of the forthcoming move. Had my brother really initiated it? Had I? Or did our parents want to, have to, move anyway? I answered these questions with a cumulative, familial yes. I knew that, in any case, my parents were more than willing to take me with them to the new place until I found an apartment and a job. There'd be no great sacrifice for them. They'd let me have the living room for a while, or the maid's room, which they intended eventually for storage. But where would I put my things and the things my parents wanted to give me? Where would I put myself, store myself?

I stared at my walls still covered with photographs and posters and shelves full of dolls, souvenirs, miniature furniture. Everything, each memory, flat or solid, seemed to be asking to escape. It was one thing for Father to talk about expansion and contraction. At his age perhaps contraction was acceptable. Not at mine.

The typewriter sat heavy on my desk, an almost human presence, like another parent, asking me to practice, whispering such sentences as *Expert advice for the quiz was given by the meek, old judge.* and *Okay, our job wages have been made equal, except for size.* —sentences no less inane than those about *quick brown foxes* and *all good men* that Mother told me she'd practiced as a child. But at least those didn't contain *Expert advice* and *job wages...* *Expert advice* with a capital *E!* I felt the weight of the words, of the typewriter itself, of the walls, the furniture, and everything in my room—a cumulative weight, crushing me. Tonight I couldn't, wouldn't again type those boring words. Like the things on the walls, I had to escape.

I stopped to say goodnight to my parents, watching television in the living room.

"I thought you were staying in," Mother said. "Where are you going at this hour?"

"To the movies."

"Which one?"

"I don't know. Whatever times right."

I watched my parents' faces sadden as they turned back to the TV screen, unable to cope with my reply which, I understood, said more about my job, my apartment, my life than about the movie—*any* movie—I was about to see.

"I think I've found it," I told them a few days later. "It's a bit expensive but really nice, really a studio apartment, not like that walk-up. Passenger elevator, service car, security system, air-conditioning—"

"You sound like a real estate broker," Father interrupted, smiling. "We can help handle the rent, if the apartment's everything you say. Let's see it."

"Yes!" Mother exclaimed, also smiling.

They both looked happier than they had in weeks, and I knew that I did too.

The building was in the former rectory of a Greenwich Village church.

"Institutions are being forced to supplement their incomes," Father remarked, as we passed heavy oak entrance doors folded in against thick stone walls, and entered the spacious lobby, cluttered with saw horses, tool boxes, and building materials.

"I see what you like about it already," Mother said. "It's so solid, not like the stuff they're building nowadays."

I led them to the passenger elevator, protected by sheets of cardboard.

"Five, please," I said to a workman who punched a button. Turning to my parents, I explained, "When more tenants are in, this will be self-service, hooked up to security."

"People living here?" Mother asked, sniffing lime and paint.

"A few. More moving in each day. It's a good deal. Free rent till the end of the year."

"Take my advice," Father said when we reached the fifth floor. "Skip the free rent. Let the dust settle. There are always problems when a building opens."

The apartment was at the southeast corner of the floor, at the end of a corridor covered with heavy brown paper, showing workmen's footprints.

"Dum-didi-dum! Dum-didi-dum!" I imitated a fanfare as I opened the door on a space about twenty feet wide, thirty-five long, with a bath and kitchen to the left of the entrance and a closet to the right. The ceiling, which started at about nine feet climbed to twelve at the windows. We all went to that end of the apartment, drawn to its height. There, from two east windows, we had a slanting view of the top of the Empire State Building, shimmering about a mile uptown. From a single window facing south, the church steeple, with a clock on it, was so near it seemed part of the apartment.

Mother leaned over the deep window sill all the way to the glass, saying, "These walls are a view in themselves. And that clock!—you'll never have an excuse for missing an appointment."

"Tick-tock! Tick-tock!" I tried, with difficulty, to repeat the rhythm of the fanfare. "Young executive climbs steeple of success. Young executive entertains clients graciously. A large desk here—" I indicated a spot at right angles to the pair of windows—"which doubles as a dining table.... Bed here." I pointed at the alcove beginning behind the kitchen. "Storage wall, screening bed." I pointed again. "And maybe, maybe, a large couch, extending from the south wall.... Please?" I looked straight at Mother, paying little attention to Father, who began to measure the room by pacing its length and width. "Please?" I repeated in the same appealing, questioning tone.

"Well," Mother answered at last, "I guess that lovely couch doesn't owe us anything, as they say. Your father and the decorator insist it won't fit in our new apartment. I could never sell it." She paused. "I'd like you to have it. I want it to stay with us."

I was hugging Mother, when Father said, "It's really too big for this room. Even if it fit, I don't know how you'd get it up here. The elevator's small. The corridor's narrow."

"The service car's big enough," I replied, surprised that, having persuaded Mother, I now had to deal with Father.

"If it is, you still have to make a turn into the corridor and then again into this apartment. Getting it into our apartment was hard. Getting it out will be hard. But getting it in here may be impossible. You'd be better off selling it and buying a smaller one, or using the one in your brother's room and spending the money from the big couch on other things you'll need."

"Daddy, please?"

"You know I'd be happy to give you the couch. I just don't want it to be a problem." He hesitated. "You can have it on two conditions: First, I want you to take its exact measurements and lay them out on a scaled plan of this apartment."

I nodded eagerly in agreement. "I know it'll work."

"Second, I want you to give the measurements to a moving company. Have them look at this building to see if they can get it in. No guessing about the size of the service car."

I nodded again and hugged Father. The couch was virtually in the apartment. I could see it, with its arms down, separating clients drinking cocktails as they watched the city darken and the Empire State Building become bright against the evening sky.

While Mother and Father prepared for their move, I reviewed my own lease with their lawyer and went with Father to the bank to arrange for monthly deposits to my account covering most of the rent.

"I'm not exactly on my own, am I?" I asked, giggling, as we left the bank.

"You will be. Meanwhile, there's one other thing I'd like you to do: show your furniture layout to our decorator."

"Daddy!"

"I know you and your mother think the couch will fit, but it's a good idea to get an outside opinion."

As I feared, the decorator thought the couch was large for the space. He also thought that, from my description, it would be very difficult to get into the building.

"Well?" Father asked that night at dinner.

I reported only on the first of the decorator's observations.

"Perhaps you'll reconsider—" Father was saying when Mother interrupted.

"Men don't understand these things. They don't understand that one kooky piece can make a room."

Father's face flushed. "All you care about is keeping that damn couch in the family. You can't let go of anything. Well, you two work it out. I don't care if you have to carry it up the fire stair." He paused, suppressing his rage. "Better have the movers check that too, just in case they can't use the elevator."

Right after Thanksgiving, a friend who had a station wagon began helping me move some of my smaller things into the apartment. Within a week I told my parents, "I can't live in two places at once. Is it okay if I take the couch? Can you do without it during your last few weeks here?"

"I'll be glad to see it go," Father replied. "But what about your building? Is the work done, the security system on?"

"Almost half the tenants are in," I exaggerated slightly. "Everything's working."

"And the movers?"

"My friend recommended an outfit called University Moving—some jocks working their way through college." Father looked dubious. "I spoke to them on the phone, gave them all the measurements. They said there'd be no problem. They've handled bigger pieces."

"They didn't look at the building?"

"Said they didn't have to, that the measurements were enough."

Once again the front door was removed from the buck. Once again the couch was placed on top of the elevator. I left saying, "I'll call tonight when I'm settled."

"Sure you don't want to have dinner with us?" Mother asked.

"You know I can't. I have to unpack. I want to stock the refrigerator. And the phone company's coming first thing in the morning."

"You shouldn't be there without a phone."

"Mother! I've got plenty of neighbors."

When I called, I think my voice must have been sadder than in weeks. "The service car's broken. The moving guys were really nice. They tried to take the couch up the stair, but they couldn't make the turn."

"Where is it?"

"In the lobby."

"Will it be safe?"

"Mother!"

During the rest of that week and into the next, I reported various frustrations and irritations: The service car still wasn't fixed. The phone wasn't receiving incom-

ing calls. The kitchen faucet leaked. Deliveries weren't
getting to me. "It's lucky I don't have a job," I finished
one conversation. "I have to be here almost all the time.
I hang around, and then the people who are supposed to
come don't."

The couch, crowded into a corner of the lobby,
seemed to age overnight. A film of plaster dust settled on
it, turning it gray. I swept it, found a plastic sheet to cover
it, waited for the elevator to be fixed. Each day as I
rushed from the apartment to do local errands and be
back in time for whoever was supposed to come, the
couch looked older, ghostly in its dusty plastic shroud.

For the second time, I gave the building superintendent a tip, begging him to help me. He put the money
in one back pocket, took a folding ruler out of the other,
carefully measured the couch, shook his head.

"The elevator should be working tomorrow, but
even if we can get it on top, you'll never get it in your
apartment. Not unless we cut off the legs. Even then—"

"The legs!"

"Yeah, they're short, but we'll have more turning
room. We can saw them carefully, so they can be put
back on."

I felt tears coming to my eyes. I nodded and
hurried out of the lobby.

When I returned, the couch was resting legless on
the lobby floor. Through the dim plastic, I could see six
stumps piled on the seat.

The superintendent and his men got the couch on
top of the service car and struggled with it for almost an
hour on the fifth floor.

"There's no way," the super told me. "The only thing —" he hesitated—"if you want us to saw it in half, you could have someone come and put it together again, and get some good material—it would look like new."

"No!" I shook my head, feeling my hair swish back and forth like a horse's tail. "Do you know what that is?" The superintendent looked mystified. "It's horsehair."

"Horse hair?" He cut the word in half, as he'd wanted to do with the couch itself. "Horse hair," he repeated slowly, "from a horse?"

I nodded. "I'll get one of the antique stores to pick it up."

That afternoon I spoke to several neighborhood dealers. "You can look at it in the lobby.... The legs can be put back on.... I'll make a reasonable deal—cash or a trade against something I can use."

When I returned, the couch, sunken and gray, was back in its corner. Until I passed the end facing me, I couldn't see the long diagonal slash in the plastic and back upholstery. Wincing, I removed a crudely printed note pinned to the plastic:

THIS DONT
BELONG HERE
SUPER

I rushed to my apartment to call him.

"I didn't write no note," the superintendent assured me. "The couch was okay when we put it back. A few tenants complained.... Or a workman might have torn it with a pipe or something.... I'll check."

In ten minutes or so my phone rang.

"Did you find out anything?" I asked before hearing Father's voice. "Oh, Daddy."

I told him most of what had happened, skipping details he could probably imagine in each pained inflection.

"I'm sorry about the couch," Father said, "but you've got to get it out of there."

"I'm trying."

"I mean, work out the price later, even give it away. Whoever did this is a psychopath. Don't provoke him."

"The super said it might have been an accident."

"Slashes aren't accidents. Notes like that aren't accidents. Maybe you should spend the night here."

"I'm all right. I'll get someone to pick it up tomorrow."

I double-locked the door, fixed dinner but couldn't eat, went to bed but couldn't sleep. I thought again and again of going down to the lobby and checking on the couch, perhaps even staying there, stretched out on it, protecting it and comforting it as it had done for me so often. Each time I started to get out of bed I remembered the "psychopath," probably lurking in the lobby, or the stair, or maybe in the corridor right outside my apartment. Who or what was this shadowy malevolence? Simply a tenant like myself, one who had gone through all the irritations of moving, of trying to get settled, and had finally reached the breaking point—the slashing point? Or was it a workman, envious of any jobless young woman who had her own apartment and could afford to leave a fancy couch unprotected in the lobby? Or—my mind was racing now, back through time, to before I was born—could it have been that German designer Father had mentioned, that man who could do anything? Was he still hobbling around, perhaps with a

sword in his cane, seeking revenge on those who ne-
glected his art? The world was moving in on me, on my
couch, the couch that I, unlike my parents, had known
my entire life.

The couch hung over my bed like an enormous
dark canopy. I felt smothered by it. How could I face
tomorrow's job interview? How, through this oppressive cloud of horsehair, could I face life itself? Would
being truly on my own remain always a little joke between Father and me? It was no consolation that he'd
never once said, "I told you so." I knew he'd thought it.

In the morning, as I came out of the elevator, I saw
the second slash, forming an awful X at the back of the
couch. A new note was pinned alongside it:

GET IT OUT
SUPER

At the bottom of the X, a triangle of plastic and horsehair
had fallen forward, exposing a gaping bulge of stuffing.

I walked quickly to the nearest antique dealer, an
elderly man who had seemed sympathetic when I'd
spoken to him the day before.

"I'll give it to you on consignment. I'll pay for
repairs. I just want it out."

He shook his head tiredly. "A piece like that's
going to take up half the store. If I put it outside, it'll get
ruined."

"Please. You have nothing to lose. I'll take the
risk. I'll pay for the trucking too."

"Okay," he said finally, "but this ain't business.
This is an old man remembering his daughter when she
was your age. I'll try to get a truck over tomorrow."

"Tomorrow! Can't you get one today?"

"Patience, my dear young lady, patience. You have your whole life ahead of you. Don't rush it. It'll go fast enough. But truckers—no. I'll be lucky if I get them for tomorrow."

Tomorrow seemed terribly far away but, as I walked to my interview, breathing the crisp December air, I already felt unburdened. My reflection in glittering store windows decorated for Christmas showed the color coming back to my cheeks. No one would have guessed I'd spent a sleepless night.

The interviewer, a chic brunette with just a touch of gray, was as nice as the dealer, the second decent person I'd seen this morning. I tried to put the couch slasher out of my mind.

"You understand, we have to spend months training someone. It's nothing you can learn overnight. We make an investment. We don't want anyone who's going to run off to another job."

"This is just what I want. I like everything I know about your company. And I like your location. I can walk here in half an hour. The worst blizzard won't stop me."

The woman smiled. "Of course I can't tell much about your habits from a college transcript, but we do expect our employees to be dependable and punctual."

"There's a clock on the church steeple right outside my apartment. I couldn't be late."

The woman smiled again. "Then you're ready to take the job?" I nodded enthusiastically. "Well, why don't we have lunch, and I'll tell you more about it. Let's tidy up while my secretary makes a reservation."

The small French restaurant was only two blocks away. The woman knew everyone there—the owner, the captain, the waiters, executives from her own company—mine now too! The food and service were perfect. I listened to the history of the company, its astonishing growth, and to the story of the woman's own success. "Maybe the starting salary's not as high as you hoped, but stay with us, and you'll be well paid." She signed the check.

I felt more excited and hopeful than since returning from Europe. The world seemed freshly wrapped, like a Christmas present. Walking down Fifth Avenue to my apartment, I wondered how many years it would be before I had a secretary and an expense account, how many Christmases before moving to a larger apartment and filling it with bright new things like those displayed in window after window. I thought of the couch only when I reached the quiet residential part of the avenue. Even then the thought was distant and elusive, not nearly as immediate as the apple tart I'd had for dessert. I could still taste it, feel its exquisite buttery texture.

From the corner of my street, I saw a fire engine parked down the block. A crowd had gathered around it, so I couldn't tell if the engine was in front of my building. As I walked more quickly toward the crowd, I could smell smoke, an increasingly heavy smell like that of burnt meat. I rushed forward, sure now that the smoke was coming from my building. A fireman stopped me.

"I live here."

"Nothing to worry about, Miss. The fire's out. Just smoldering."

"Where?" But I knew the answer. I was sure.

"In the lobby. Some nut left a piece of furniture there."

"And some nut set it on fire?"

"Yeah, probably."

I went around the engine to the other side of the entrance where the super was standing. "How did it happen?"

"Who knows?" He shrugged. "Maybe someone was careless with a cigarette. Maybe someone used a match."

I listened without speaking while the firemen reeled in the hose, slithering and clanking across the sidewalk.

"Some mess," the super said, when we entered the lobby.

The couch was unrecognizable. Limp springs protruded from bits of charred frame resting in a pool of muddy ashes. The couch's stench lingered in the air— not burnt meat but hair. I turned away from the super and began to cry as I left the building. Farther outside I wiped my eyes and blew my nose before starting on my way to the antique dealer to call off our deal. With each step, I sniffled less, felt lighter, had a stronger sense that, no matter how much I had loved the couch, no matter how irresponsibly I had loved it, I was finally on my own. Almost on my own.

Between the Flags

"Want to drive down to the beach?" His bathing suit and sports shirt were damp with perspiration. "Get a breath of air?"

"Too much to do here." His wife pointed out at the garden. "You go. Have a good time."

Her silver hair, a slightly tarnished halo, shimmered in the intense light coming through the clerestory.

"We won't stay long. An hour at most."

"No, you go. Go without me."

Again he looked at her hair. Was it why she didn't want to come? The ocean did something to it, she often said. Or, if not the salt in the sea, the chlorine in the pool. Always some reason not to swim.

"We're only having drinks with the Hortons. Suppose your hair isn't perfect?"

"My hair's the least of it. The sun's still high. I can't wear a hat in the ocean." She smiled, put on her gardening hat, glanced at herself in the mirror. "And I can't stand what's happening to my skin."

He studied her studying herself. The brim of the hat cast a shadow over her face, softening wrinkles, caused surely by laughter as much as by worry. Their forty years of laughter and worry. He bent under the hat and kissed her cheek.

"Your skin's beautiful. Nobody could guess your age. Come on. In and out."

"You don't understand. Men age better."

"Do we?"

"Well, it shows less." She returned his kiss, then repeated, "You go. Go now, or we'll be late for the Hortons." She handed him a towel and walked with him to the garage. "If the water's cold, don't stay in too long. You don't have to prove anything. And don't sneak a lot of cigarettes. You've had two or three since lunch."

Five, he remembered, as he lit the sixth on the way to the beach—she didn't know about the two in the bathroom. He dragged deeply and exhaled, liking how the smoke was pulled out of the open car window, almost as if directly out of his lungs, flushing them, even cooling them.

There was room at the near end of the parking lot, but he drove on toward the ocean, hoping he'd find a better spot and resenting every parked car he passed. Then there it was, a space right up front, probably just vacated by someone who'd had too much sun. The space was next to two empty ones marked with thin blue stick figures—bare bones—in wheelchairs. On the other side, a stocky boy standing in the bed of a pick-up truck was handing surfboards and wet-suits to three friends, shouting, "What waves! Man, they're really mean! Bad-ass monster mothers!"

The boys were unloading a cooler as he walked to the edge of the beach, feeling he'd parked just where he belonged, in a sort of retirement slot—a compulsory retirement slot—between old age and youth. Closer to old age, where the empty blue silence was at least a language he could understand.

Next to the Village sign disclaiming responsibility to bathers, there might just as well have been another forbidding the beach to those over sixty-five. Everyone was young—two fellows spinning around as they glided a frisbee back and forth; two others, on the run, passing a football; a couple playing paddleball; mothers with children digging in the sand; slightly older kids dancing in and out of the surf; and, farther out, to the right of the swimming area, surfers poised elegantly on their boards. Even the litter on the beach—more than there used to be—looked young: cans, cartons, publications, all with new names, names he didn't know, this year's names written in the sand. He glanced up, half expecting to see still more garbage floating in the sky. Gulls soared throughout the pale purple haze. They looked athletic, if not young.

He was close to the lifeguards' stand when the football came toward him, falling fast. He lunged, trying to catch it on the fly; missed; at the first bounce, lunged again; missed again. The ball settled in the sand, and he picked it up.

The intended receiver, muscles bulging and covered with sweat, ran up to him and took the ball.

"Nice try," the boy yelled over his shoulder, heaving a perfect pass to his friend forty or fifty yards down the beach.

One lifeguard was on top of the stand, seated beside a blue flag. A second was on the beach, practicing a martial arts regimen of stretches and flexes.

"Guard!" he called to the one on top. "Guard!"

The fellow finally looked down.

"Blue means caution, doesn't t it?" *Bad-ass monster mothers* still roared through his mind.

"That's it. Just stay between the flags." The guard made a quick gesture, encompassing two fluttering scraps of yellow. "Don't go out too far."

The guard's side of the conversation was totally predictable; his own, totally false. Well, maybe not totally. What he had wanted to say was, "keep an eye on me." Maybe he had. In a way. In code. But if he'd said, "I'm not as young as I used to be," even that wouldn't have been what he was really thinking, specifically thinking: that not so many years ago he used to swim straight out, maybe half a mile, before starting back; that now he went only just past the breakers and swam short laps, always parallel to the shore, always between the flags, between the flags, between the flags, until he was winded.

Using the breeze to spread his towel, he lowered it onto a smooth stretch of sand, tossed his shirt on the towel, his sandals on the shirt. All of this had become a ritual, ever since an afternoon long ago, when his shirt, with car keys, cigarettes and matches in the pocket, had blown far down the beach, spilling everything along the way. The same beach, a lot cleaner then. A similar shirt, anonymous, without a logo. Keys for a different car, an American car in those days, the black Buick that had given him over 100,000 miles. And Camels. Always Camels. Since the navy in World War II. Before business. Before marriage. Before children. Before grandchildren.... As he walked to the water's edge, he tried to recapture that distant afternoon: offering the children a quarter each for finding the shirt, the keys, the cigarettes that didn't even cost a quarter then; the children's triumphant return with everything, including the matches, which cost him an extra quarter; the drive to the penny-candy store....

The water must have been in the low sixties, no more than that. It snapped him back into the present, the world of his forced retirement, of grown children, of grandchildren, of dollar rewards and shrunken candy bars at five times the old price, of toys, of head-shop paraphernalia, and God only knew what else, sold at so-called candy stores. The rollers rushed over his ankles, up to his calves, his knees. He bent for a moment, never taking his eyes off the waves, while splashing himself and adjusting to the water. For the first time since this morning he was comfortably cool.

He stood up, bracing himself for the next rollers. They looked larger now than they had from shore. He turned sideways, taking as little as possible of their impact, moving forward through the spray, waiting for the right wave, the kind he had been diving under for more than sixty years. The undertow was tugging at his feet and legs when the wave came, building to a clean peak, maybe ten feet high. He timed it perfectly, pushed forward from the bottom, dove deep, felt the wave rush over him, heard its parting roar.

Surfacing, he began swimming through the choppy sea toward the breakers farther out. After them, everything would be easier, smoother. Despite the ocean's vastness, surrounding him, supporting and attacking him, as always he also felt its intimacy, connecting him with both an ancient piscine history and with future generations—children behind him, playing on the beach; surfers ahead of him, riding distant waves.

The next breaker stood twice the height of the previous one. It rolled toward him, becoming larger and larger, opening its concave face wider and wider. He prepared to dive, again feeling for the bottom to push himself forward. Suddenly the ocean was bottomless, and the wave hung above him. He plunged into a tunnel of air, not reaching the wave but falling beneath it and swimming hard to get underwater. Holding his breath, listening, hoping the wave had passed over him, he came up for air just as it broke. Its enormous weight struck, forcing him down again. He was on the bottom now, being tossed and dragged over rough sand. He felt the water grab his bathing suit and take it down to his ankles. He was reaching for it, trying to pull it back on, when he was tossed again and fell tumbling and scraping farther and farther along the bottom.

For a single turbulent moment he could see himself, as if from above, on the floor of the ocean, helplessly twisting and turning. At that moment, he knew, he could *see*, how insignificant he was, how little it mattered if he lived or died, how much better this death was than the deaths of friends who had thrashed through *their* forced retirements with little to do but fight the diseases that destroyed their hearts and minds, their lungs and vital organs. He gasped for air, swallowed water, was tempted by the ease with which the ocean made him a part of itself, continuing to drag him along toward some deep comfortable grave.

As if helping to dig that grave, he dug his feet into the sand. This broke his drift, and the sea did the rest, lifting him almost to a standing position. As he pushed off the bottom, he felt the fatigue in his legs and then in his arms, barely able to paddle in small circles. His heart pounded. His lungs burned. He needed air.

He had no idea how long it took to reach the surface or just where he was when he reached it. For a minute he bobbed blindly, catching his breath and trying not to swallow more water. He was frightened and sick to his stomach. His skin stung where it had been scraped. His heart still pounded, his lungs still burned, his arms and legs were still hard to lift.

The ocean stretched for miles toward a dim horizon. On the next swell he turned and saw a somewhat sharper shoreline, spotted with beach cottages. Though dazed, he realized that he had drifted parallel to the shore, that it wasn't more than twenty-five yards away, and that just past the cottages, two dancing patches of yellow flanked a higher one of blue.

Inside the line of breakers, the undertow was strong. He did his best to duck under large waves and ride smaller ones, saving what strength he had left to fight the undertow. Moving a few yards forward, being carried a few back, his progress was slow, his breath short, his arms and legs heavier than ever. He tried to touch bottom, hoping that he could hold his position and that soon he could walk ashore. The bottom was still out of reach.

There were moments when he almost quit, almost blacked out; moments when, as in that single one at the bottom of the sea, he knew he had a choice. Once, long ago in the navy, he had almost fallen asleep on watch, almost given in. If he had, he knew now, the navy would have been right to court-martial him, right to hold him responsible, right to recognize he had made a decision, right... He shook his head, surprised that, as he rose and fell with the sea, he wasn't aboard ship; surprised, too, the navy and its then seemingly harsh code were what he now remembered. For years he'd heard that, during the moments preceding death people's entire lives flashed before them. But, on the bottom, nothing had flashed, nothing but himself, completely alone, tangled in his bathing suit, trying to save it rather than his life.... Nothing. Not a single biographical flash. No childhood. No parents. No grandparents. No siblings. No school. No college. No navy. No early years in business. No late years, either, gradually stripped of responsibility and then, at sixty-five, trying to find another job. No years beyond that—two, almost three—of feeling useless. No marriage. No children. No grandchildren. Nothing. Nothing then that was in his mind now. But perhaps then, just a few minutes ago, he wasn't ready. Perhaps it was that simple. Not being ready. Or, more positively— perhaps more positively—being unready, being truly unready for the flash.

Strange that, with the fight almost won, with the shore closer and closer, he was more ready now—more hopelessly exhausted, anyway. Again he was tempted to quit, to black out. Again he wondered why he was struggling, what he was struggling toward, swimming toward. Again he tried to touch bottom. He could feel it there now, at the tips of his toes. He lifted one numb arm, then the other. With the help of a roller and a few more strokes, he could almost walk. He fell forward, half riding a wave, half dog-paddling, and crawled, exhausted and confused, onto the beach.

For several minutes he stayed there on his stomach, as his heart pounded and he gasped for air. The water, lapping at his body, was cold but soothing. Scrapes and cuts tingled, coming to life. His heartbeat and breathing slowed slightly, only slightly. At last he wobbled to his feet and, as if awaking from a dream, walked slowly toward the flags, the lifeguards' stand, his towel, his cigarettes.

There was, he knew, something absurd about wanting a cigarette—his lungs still burned—but for now it was as far into the future as he could think. Yet, after a dozen more steps through the heavy sand, he began thinking further ahead. Despite lingering nausea—part salt, part fear—what he wanted next was a martini. As soon as possible. Even before going to the Hortons. With that wish, his catalogue of desires abruptly ended. Abruptly retired.

In front of him, several mothers were playing with their children. As he approached, he saw the nearest young woman's expression change suddenly from contentment to something like disgust or horror, something vaguely incomprehensible and uncomprehending.

"Oh, God!" she started to shriek. "Oh-h-h —" The exclamation became a muted moan.

She covered one child's eyes while turning away the face of another. The other mothers stifled their screams too and played more busily with their children, obviously not wanting them to look.

He examined the scratches on his legs, felt them, expecting his hands to be covered with blood. There was very little, surely not enough to frighten anyone. It was only then, as his hands moved up from his thighs to his groin, that he realized he had lost his bathing suit.

He wanted to run for his towel, took a few strides, and stopped. He was panting again, his heart pounded, he couldn't run, he couldn't even walk any faster than before. Breathing hard, he continued slowly across the beach. He had nearly reached the towel before understanding that, no matter what these young mothers thought, no matter what anyone thought, they didn't know, couldn't know, just how naked he really was.